FACE TO FACE

McGruder nosed his horse into the porch rail. "Where's the sonuvabitch?"

"I ain't got no hired hands here," Corely said. "Couldn't afford 'em if I wanted to. You murdered the only help I ever had." His voice quavered, losing some of its strength.

Ollfinger stiffened. "A man shouldn't make accusations with no proof."

McGruder broke in again. "Where is he? I owe him."

"You mean Ketcham? I don't know. He ain't a hired hand. Just a man passing through."

McGruder shot a glance around the place, then back at Corely. "You're hiding him."

Ketcham had heard enough and stepped around the corner. Their hands moved for their guns. His Winchester came up.

"You want me, McGruder?"

KETCHAM'S LAND

DOUGLAS HIRT

LEISURE BOOKS NEW YORK CITY

For Pat and Susan Weaver

LEISURE BOOKS®

August 2002

Published by

Dorchester Publishing Co., Inc.
276 Fifth Avenue
New York, NY   10001

ISBN: 0-8439-5033-1

Visit us on the web at www.dorchesterpub.com.

KETCHAM'S LAND

Chapter One

Chance Ketcham slid his winnings off the table and into his pouch with one eye on Gellerman. The man was tighter than a roped calf and hotter than the iron. Ketcham watched to see if he was fool enough to draw. Gellerman had just enough distilled lightning in him to try. He'd already commented on Ketcham's "luck." Now was the time to reap that luck and leave, though his own legs were none too steady.

Gellerman hitched back his chair, his cold blue eyes glaring. "Where you going?"

"It's getting late." Ketcham made his voice easy as his view circled the table. They'd all been drinking heavily, but the cards had fallen his way for a change. The kid, Haseltine, had dropped

1

some pretty heavy change into Ketcham's pot, too. Haseltine snatched up his glass and drained the red-eye. Harold Reed's luck had run dry like the others. He eyed Ketcham beneath liquor-laden eyelids.

"Give us a chance to win some of it back, Chance," Reed said.

"Another night, boys."

Gellerman's narrowing eyes didn't waver. "Your kind of luck comes from an extra ace hidden somewhere."

Ketcham stiffened.

Gellerman's hand lowered toward his six-shooter.

Ketcham's head cleared, his brain instantly sobering from the whiskey. "You ready to back up those words, Gellerman?"

Benny Gellerman had drifted into Bailey about a year earlier and signed on with the Muleshoe outfit. Ketcham never much liked the man. Word had it he was on the run, though no one was ever fool enough to ask. Something had happened in the Territories and he'd hightailed it over the border into Texas. Ketcham knew no more than that, except that Gellerman had a hair-trigger temper and lightning-quick fists.

"I say you cheated." Gellerman stood.

The Cattle King Saloon went silent. Over by the bar, Jorge Rodriguez set down his glass and moved to one side. Ketcham had at least one friend here.

He grinned. "You're drunk, Benny. That's the whiskey talking." His view slid toward the batwings. There'd be no easy way out of the saloon with Gellerman like this—but it wouldn't be the first time. Well, there was one way. His grin widened out into a smile and he stepped closer to Gellerman. Without warning, Ketcham's fist jerked up.

Gellerman folded at the waist, his breath exploding. But as if reading Ketcham's next move, Gellerman went to one side, avoiding the knuckles that reached for his chin.

Haseltine and Reed leaped back as the table crashed aside. Gellerman came around with a left hook that missed, at the same time jerking his revolver from its holster.

Ketcham's boot snapped out and kicked the gun from his hand. He swung a fist into Gellerman's side. The man staggered, grabbed for a chair, and broke it against a post where Ketcham had been standing. The two circled. Ketcham shot a left and followed instantly with a right uppercut. Gellerman slammed into the piano and Ketcham dove in, pounding the man to his knees.

When it was over, Ketcham staggered back. No one moved. Haseltine and Reed stepped out of his way as he swooped his pouch from the floor.

"Game's over, boys." He grinned.

Near the bar, Rodriguez gave a slight nod. Ketcham returned a wry smile to his friend, then,

3

grabbing his hat from the floor, made his way for the batwings.

"I'll get you, Ketcham!" Gellerman called, standing with the help of three or four of his friends. "Yeah, you'd better run!"

Ketcham ignored him, stepped out into the night, and climbed onto his horse. As he rode away, he wondered if maybe the time had come to pull out. This part of West Texas was getting a mite crowded for his liking. There was always something better over the next hill. Someplace still open and wild where a man like him could leave his mark. Now that it was over, the whiskey fog began to creep back into his brain.

Ketcham rode out into the dark prairie to his campsite. He'd quit the Muleshoe outfit a week earlier, so why was he still hanging around Bailey? He tied off his horse, not bothering to unsaddle it, staggered to his bedroll, and fell asleep almost at once.

How many hours passed before he heard the soft approach of a horse from the darkness, he had know way of knowing. His eyes snapped open, aching from the whiskey still in his brain. His hand inched toward his gun as the animal came closer. He yanked it free and spun toward the noise.

"It is only me, *mi amigo*!"

"Rodriguez?"

Beneath the faint moonlight, horse and rider emerged from the darkness. Ketcham released a breath and lowered the hammer of his Colt. He licked his lips, feeling shoe leather instead of skin.

"What are you doing sneaking around here? Don't you know that can get you killed?"

"I take the chance. I didn't know where you were—not exactly. You sleep in a lonely place, *mi amigo*."

"I don't like unexpected visitors. Light off that horse, Jorge. I'll build a fire and make us some coffee. Lord, I could use a cup."

Rodriguez remained mounted, looking worried.

"What is it?"

"There is no time for that, *mi amigo*. Gellerman."

"What about Gellerman?"

"After you leave, he call his *amigos* together. They drink a lot of whiskey. They are more than just a leetle drunk now, and now they come to find you."

"How many?"

"Seven, last I see them. That *el muchacho*, Haseltine, he is with him."

"Reed?"

Rodriguez shook his head. "Reed not with them."

Ketcham drew in a breath, held it a moment, then let go. "I've been figuring it's time to move on."

"Where will you go?"

He shrugged. "West. Someplace where there's space to breathe." He began breaking camp.

Rodriguez nodded. "If you must, then go quickly." He looked around. "They can't be too far behind me."

Ketcham packed up his bedroll with what few cooking utensils he owned, and as he swung up onto his horse, both he and Rodriguez heard a sound.

"Don't move too quiet, do they?" Ketcham pointed to the dark ridge a few hundred yards off. A line of riders had momentarily skylined themselves against the moon.

"They are very drunk."

Ketcham grimaced. "Thanks for the warning, Rodriguez."

"Will I see you again, *mi amigo*?"

He frowned. "Who knows?" But in his heart he doubted they ever would. They shook hands.

"I'll go talk to them. Keep them busy while you find that new land, Ketcham. *Via con Dios*."

Ketcham was two hours out of Bailey, with the dawn still an hour away at his back, when he finally crossed over into the Territories. The road ahead was clear and his horse surefooted, as the night faded and the first gray streaks of daylight began to brighten the sky.

At Riley's Switch he reined in the plucky mare and let her drink from an irrigation ditch on the west side of the tracks. Riley's Switch was no more than a run-down railroad siding, but the farmers had found this place, too. Like a blight upon the land, they were busy busting up the range and planting cotton and peanuts. Barbed wire ran along the dusty road where his horse stood breathing hard. Times were changing. Texas was being tamed—even the Territories now. It *was* time for him to move on. What had happened back in Bailey only helped to make up his mind sooner.

He rolled a smoke and considered his direction; any one that took him away from civilization would suit him just fine.

He got the horse moving again, easy now, and turned her south on a rutted track scratched into the red New Mexico dirt. Morning stretched out and the sun burned hot on his shoulders. He took off his hat, wiped the sweat from his forehead and from the hatband, and settled it back in place. His spurs moved the animal into an easy canter. She responded to the slightest pressure, as if reading his thoughts as well as his spurs.

The blazing sun had baked the dry land into powder that clung to his sweating cheeks and hands. The horse turned a shade lighter, and Ketcham tasted the gritty New Mexico clay on his teeth. Sweat stung the corners of his eyes.

The morning became noon, and noon pushed shadows out behind him as the day wore on. He kept to the west when the rut he was following forked. In a little while he swung wide and came

7

around on the east side of Portales Springs. From afar he studied the caves where the spring flowed from. No one was about, but the place was littered with the cast-offs of other travelers like himself. He'd heard that a man named Doak Good had once lived in the caves. But that had been a while back, when Good had first come to this Territory. He'd moved on since.

He watered his horse at the spring and let her crop a patch of dry grass while he took his Winchester out a ways and flipped over a rangy jack that had burst from a clump of sage. He left the skin and entrails for the coyotes and turned the pink meat over a small fire until it was brown and sizzling.

After tightening the cinches, he mounted up in the shank of the day and continued west, dozing in the saddle, coming awake from time to time as night drew on. His horse plodded along untended. It was full dark when he finally saw the lights in the distance and drew rein near a hummock of black mesquite. How far had he come?

Those far-off lights were likely from a farmer's house. Lots of sodbusters were filling this part of the Territory. His horse was flagging. She needed water and good grass hay. Trusting to her night vision, he reined off the road and headed for the lights. The house sat back a half mile, down a pair of wagon ruts, and a dog barked when he drew up in the yard.

Behind curtained windows a shadow moved.

Someone carried a lamp into another room. Light showed briefly against the curtains there, then brightened toward the door, but almost at once the flame was snuffed. The door opened a crack and a man's voice spoke from the darkness.

"What do you want, mister?"

The dog stood off a few paces, yapping and making quick runs at the horse's hind hooves.

"I've been traveling all day. Got a tired animal. Was hoping you could spare some grain and hay. I'd appreciate you letting me sleep in your barn."

For a moment the man said nothing. "What's your name?"

"Ketcham. Chance Ketcham."

The door parted and an old man stepped out cradling a scattergun in the crook of his right arm. He looked Ketcham over intently in the little bit of light coming from the window behind him. "Where you from, Mr. Ketcham, and where you bound?"

"I drift around some. Last night I spread my bedroll outside of Bailey."

"Bailey? That's a far piece of riding." The old man studied him more. Ketcham could see that his good sense and his sense of doing good were wrestling with each other. Then he came to a decision. "I'll get a light and show you the way."

"Thanks." He started out of the saddle, but the dog growled and charged his heel.

"King! Enough of that! Away with you."

9

The dog broke off and trotted into the shadows. The old man went back inside, and Ketcham lighted upon the ground and stretched, hearing his spine crackle. It felt good to arch and reach. The old man returned a moment later carrying a lantern. Its yellow light showed a long, bony face with a scattering of gray hair atop. It was a worried face. But more important, Ketcham figured, the lamp showed him Ketcham's own face, and the man seemed to relax a little.

Leading the way, the oldster took him back to a corral gate. The corral came off the side of a rickety barn that leaned considerably, and even in the deep shadows it appeared to be fair game for the next big dust devil to come along.

Ketcham unsaddled the mare and turned her loose in the corral. She found the water and hay, and the two men stood watching her eat.

"There's a currycomb inside." The old man inclined his bony head at the barn.

"Thanks."

He showed Ketcham into the barn and pointed to a pile of hay in a corner that would be his bed. Ketcham slung the saddle atop an empty stall rail and paused to probe the deep shadows. There were no animals. Whatever stock the old man owned must have been kept someplace other than this dilapidated horse shed.

"Come to the house. The daughter-in-law's got a kettle on, and there's leftover stew in the pot. Oh, by the by, my name is Corely Mattlin."

They shook hands. Taking the rifle and saddle-bags, Ketcham followed Corely to the house, but stopped at a pump and worked the handle. He smelled of sweat and old whiskey, and the thought of going into a house where a lady was made him keenly aware of himself. He shucked his shirt and scrubbed quickly under the flow. There wasn't much he could do to clean the shirt, and he reluctantly shoved his arms back into the sleeves. Corely waited for him. The cold water had shocked him awake some, but he was still walking dead on his feet, and thinking of that pile of hay back in the barn.

Three split logs served as steps up to a porch, and the door swung open on wooden hinges. They entered a cozy room with a stove on one side and a table near the wall by a window. A counter for cutting and preparing food ran partway along one wall. Two straight-back chairs, an old rocker with threadbare cushions, and a hutch holding a few dishes filled up the rest of the room. The floor was of milled planks with lots of spring to them. A big oval rug covered about half the floor. A fireplace took up half the north wall, but it had no fire burning this time of the year. Two doors to Ketcham's left might have led to bedrooms. They were both closed, and he couldn't be sure. Although small and plain, the house appeared clean and looked after.

A woman, considerably younger than Corely, was bent by the stove chucking splits from a tin wood bin into the firebox. She straightened, quickly brushing her hands on the apron that covered her brown skirt, then lifted the lid off an iron pot and stirred it with a wooden spoon.

"My daughter-in-law, Margaret Mattlin."

"Ma'am." He remembered his upbringing and swept his hat from his head.

She turned and smiled briefly.

"This here is Mr. Ketcham," Corely said.

"Mr. Ketcham." Margaret Mattlin was a slender woman, tall and gangling. Her young, plain face already showed the effects of the sun and wind and hard work. "I'll have your plate ready in a few minutes." She turned back to stirring the pot.

"Much obliged."

Corely waved him to a chair at the table. Ketcham leaned the rifle in a corner and set the saddlebags by it. Corely filled two cups from a coffeepot on the stove and the men sat across from each other.

"Been drier than usual." Corely watched him over the brim of his cup as he took a drink.

He nodded. "Ditches appear low."

Corely frowned. "In some places. We're dryland here."

"Hard way to scratch out a living." He tasted the coffee. It had been sitting in the pot too long, but right then he didn't mind.

"We make out okay, Mr. Ketcham."

From the stove, Mrs. Mattlin mumbled quietly, "When folks leave us alone."

Corely shot her a glance, quickly looking back at Ketcham so he wouldn't notice. "Any news from over Bailey way?"

"Nothing much." He hitched his head at the darkened window. "What do folks farm around here?"

"Sweet potatoes mostly, and some peanuts. What is it you do in Bailey, Mr. Ketcham?"

Now wasn't the time to raise hackles. If he admitted to being a cowman, he'd earn this stranger's ire before he'd laid his head to hay. He'd seen too much bad blood between wranglers and sodbusters to doubt that.

"I don't do anything in Bailey. I was just passing through. Before that, I hauled freight. Usually to and from the AT and Santa Fe station in Liberty. I used to have a wagon and a team, and I did all right for a while moving hardware and fencing." That wasn't entirely untrue. He'd driven a freight wagon a few years back and knew enough about the business to talk intelligently about it, and that was all. "But then I started getting itchy feet." He grinned.

Corely looked him up and down, his gray eyes lingering a moment upon Ketcham's six-shooter. "I'd have pegged you for some other line of work."

Mrs. Mattlin stopped fussing at the stove and stared even harder than Corely.

13

Ketcham cleared his throat. "What other work?"

"I don't know. A cowpuncher, maybe." He made it sound casual, but there was accusation hidden in his words.

Ketcham laughed. "Well, I've put my hand to just about everything. Still waitin' for the one that calls my name."

A grin made a brief appearance on Corely's long face, pushing aside three or four days' growth of gray bristle on his chin.

Mrs. Mattlin didn't smile. The chill in her look knifed through him and made him think quickly over his words. Nothing offensive that he could tell. She clanked a spoon inside the iron pot on the stove and set a bowl of stew on the table in front of him. "Here you are, Mr. Ketcham. Hope it's to your liking."

"Yes, ma'am. Smells real good." Not even his compliment brought her smile back.

She placed a basket of crusty bread on the table, and he tackled the victuals like a man about three-quarters starved—which wasn't too far from the truth. The stew was tasty, and it filled up that empty place behind his belt buckle. When he'd finally sopped up the last of the juice, Corely's thoughts had moved on, which was fine by him. The old man was by the window, peeling back a curtain and staring out into the black night.

"I'd be pleased to help out some around here, for your hospitality, and for what me and my animal have eaten."

"No need to. I'd not turn away a stranger in need."

"Just the same, I'd like to help." He checked Mrs. Mattlin for a smile and thought he saw some softening to her features. Could have been the light, though.

Corely pursed his lips, giving Mrs. Mattlin a glance. "Whal, I reckon there are a few chores around here a young, strong man such as yourself might take a lick at. We can talk about it in the morning."

Ketcham left it at that. "Well, thanks for your kindness and the good food." He collected his rifle and saddlebags. "Guess I'll turn in."

Now Mrs. Mattlin did force a smile. "I hope you will be comfortable enough."

"Yes, ma'am." He'd be a sight more comfortable anywhere outside her scrutiny.

He heard the latch being thrown behind him as he stepped outside into a pleasant night. The moon had yet to rise very high, and the faint light from the window showed little of the property. With the dog, King, sniffing his heels, he made his way to the barn. A breeze whispered softly through the branches of a dark stand of cottonwoods off to his right. The far-off yapping of coyotes came drifting in from the sand hills. The night would be pleasant for sleeping.

Inside the barn he yanked off his boots, placed his revolver at hand, curled up in his blanket upon a nest of hay, and was immediately asleep.

Chapter Two

The squeaking of the pump handle dragged Ketcham from a deep sleep. The sun was already high in the sky. How had he slept so late? Then he recalled his long ride from Bailey, and finally coming upon this lone homestead in the dark. A wry grin tightened his lips. He threw off the blanket and sat up, grinding his knuckles into the small of his back. He stretched and reached for his boots.

Outside, Mrs. Mattlin was filling a pot at the pump.

"Morning, Mrs. Mattlin."

She watched him stroll up from the corral gate. "Mr. Ketcham. You look like the sleep did you good."

"Did I look all that done in?"

She smiled, which prettied up her face considerably. "You were moving on sheer determination and not much else last night."

He grinned.

"I've saved breakfast for you, and there's a fresh pot of coffee brewing." She took up her bucket and went back into the house. She cut a fine figure in a beige skirt and cotton shirtwaist. Ketcham wondered if she always dressed so nicely to do chores. He found himself staring long after she'd disappeared into the house.

The cold well water washed the sleep from his eyes and took the taste of it from his mouth. But it did nothing to take the odor from his clothes. He'd have to do laundry soon. Plastering his unruly hair down with a hand, he frowned and wished for the comb he'd left back in his saddlebags. Levering his hat over his wet hair, he started for the house thinking Corely and Mrs. Mattlin's husband would be inside. But they weren't. It was strange he hadn't seen any signs of Mrs. Mattlin's husband.

The smell of breakfast fixings was a little bit like paradise . . . paradise the way his folks used to paint it. He grimaced at the memory and shoved it out of his mind.

Mrs. Mattlin was at the counter scrubbing dishes in a big pail. She paused only long enough to fix him a plate of warm eggs, potatoes, and bacon from a Dutch oven on the stove.

Ketcham looked around. "Your father-in-law not here?" *Or your husband?* he almost asked.

"Corely's out bringing in the team." She set the plate on the table and filled a tin cup from the coffeepot on the stove.

He'd guessed the animals had been put out to pasture. There'd been no sign of any livestock in or about the barn. "Maybe I ought to go help him."

"Help who?" The door closed behind Corely Mattlin and he hung his straw hat on a peg near the shotgun Ketcham had met the night before.

"You. Mrs. Mattlin just said you were bringing in stock from pasture."

"Already got 'em out front." Corely filled a cup for himself, then lingered a few moments by the window, peering out from time to time through a slit in the curtains as he sipped it.

Ketcham ate his breakfast, and between bites offered again to take on some chores to pay back their kindness. Corely abandoned the window and settled into the chair across the table. "You're just all fired up to help us out."

"Least I can do."

He considered a moment, his eyes fixed on something between Ketcham's head and the ceiling. "Fair enough. How are you at swinging an ax?"

"I've cut a fair share of timber in my days. Won't claim to be Paul Bunyan, but I can lay in a stack of winter wood with the best of them."

Margaret said, "What about moving on? Drifting men don't usually hang long in one place."

"I'm in no hurry, ma'am." He smiled, but she did not.

"How are you behind a plow?"

"Not very good. Never had any reason to learn." That wasn't exactly true. He'd had plenty of time to learn, growing up on his folks' farm back in Arkansas. But he hadn't liked their farming any more than he cared for their religion— one of many reasons he'd struck out on his own more than a dozen years earlier.

"Want to learn?"

"Only if plowing is where you need help." He could be as stubborn as any cowman. The idea of busting up good grazing land to plant potatoes and peanuts rankled. But being a "freighter," he couldn't let it show.

Corely gave a short laugh. "I won't twist your arm."

"Then I'll lay in two cords of firewood in trade for a few days' resting up here and some more of Mrs. Mattlin's good cooking."

Mrs. Mattlin cast an appreciative smile over her shoulder.

Corely considered, then nodded. "Sounds fair enough. My shoulders don't move like they once did, and sometimes I get my back thrown out, or I'd have seen to the job already."

Ketcham wondered briefly why his son hadn't done the chore for the old man. But he didn't know these folks well enough to ask personal questions like that.

Mrs. Mattlin finished her scrubbing and disappeared through one of the doors. She came back a few minutes later with a knit bag over her arm. She paused to consider and then adjust the angle of a straw sunbonnet in a small mirror hanging next to two framed tintypes on the wall between the doors.

Corely's chair scraped back and he set his cup on the counter. "Me and Margaret got to go into town today, Mr. Ketcham. Want to ride along?"

The way he said it made it plain he didn't want to leave a stranger alone in his house while they were away.

"What town's nearby?"

"Carson. It's about three miles west of here."

He'd never been to Carson, never been this far west anywhere inside the Territories. "I'll ride along."

Catching a glimpse of his image in the mirror as he strode past, he frowned at the face that looked back at him, more gaunt than the last time he remembered seeing it. The brown eyes sat deeper in their sockets, and a stubbly shadow darkened its chin. He needed a shave as well as a bath.

Mrs. Mattlin gathered up a bundle of bright wildflowers from the counter: reds, purples, and yellows. Ketcham didn't know the names of all of them. They had been fresh picked and looked somehow out of place in the drab little house.

A pair of dun swayback nags hitched to a gray wagon waited out front. Corely helped Margaret up onto the seat. Ketcham said he'd be a moment, and King sniffed at his legs and romped around him all the way back to the barn, where he fetched his six-shooter and holster off the top of the nail keg where he'd put it the night before. On the way back he lobbed a stick. The dog chased it across the corral and brought it back. There must have been a seep to the east of the barn where a dense stand of cottonwood trees grew. The thought passed from his brain as he hauled back and let the stick sail high and far, and land among those trees.

Mrs. Mattlin watched him return to the wagon. Maybe she was staring at the holstered revolver slung over his shoulder. He couldn't read her expression. He hopped over the wagon box, shoved the revolver into the corner among some empty burlap feed sacks, and settled down against the side boards. King dropped the stick by the wheel, and his tail drooped as Corely turned the wagon out of the yard and onto the two ruts Ketcham had followed up the night before.

He hadn't noticed it in the dark, but the road skirted a hoed field where rows and rows of low, green plants gave the dry land an almost unnatural hue. A single strand of barbed wire stretched between spindly posts was all that kept beasts larger than a dog out of his truck patch. Like the barn, the loose wire looked to be fair game for the next strong wind or headstrong cow.

"Sweet potatoes?"

"Uh-huh." Corely kept his eyes directed ahead. The wagon rumbled on until it came to the main road. He turned left and the house and fields disappeared in the distance against the drab greens and browns of the land.

He tried to find a comfortable position in the wagon box, listening to the creak and groan of wood and leather, and the steady plodding of the horses. The day was heating up, and dust hung in the hot air and clung to his skin. Dust seemed to be as much a part of this Eastern New Mexico Territory as the cactus and rattlesnakes.

There wasn't much difference between here and West Texas, where he'd come from. He had heard it claimed that one day the winds would blow New Mexico into Texas, and the next day they'd blow Texas back into New Mexico. It seemed both places were only borrowing each other's dirt. He grinned, thinking that if them Yankee bankers and lawyers ever got wind of what was happening down here, they'd figure out a way to charge interest on all that borrowed dirt.

About half a mile along the road they passed another house set far back and surrounded by potato fields and wire. He realized he was frowning. This part of the country was surely filling up. Where would a man like himself, who fancied

22

open spaces, go? Maybe Montana. Maybe the Dakotas. Arizona was still pretty wide open, but Colorado was crowding up fast; Denver City already had more than twenty thousand folks living in it. Twenty thousand! It strained his head to imagine so many people packed all together in one place.

"We'll not linger long?" Corely asked Mrs. Mattlin at one point.

"Got to dig up the old," she replied.

"Susan's been tending them."

"Not today."

He nodded, then after a pause asked, "When is Betia due?"

"Any day now."

It was small talk—family talk—snatches of a common life, and it made a stranger like himself realize just how much of an outsider he really was. But then, that's the lot of a drifter. Always the outsider. He frowned and pulled his hat down over his eyes. He was still trying to get comfortable when he sniffed the air. He sniffed again—no mistaking the smell of cows. Lots of cows.

"What the devil?" Corely declared.

Mrs. Mattlin made a low sound that might have been concern, or disappointment, or worry. Ketcham sat up and tipped his hat back. The road ahead was shadowed with cows, thicker than warts on a toad. Riders had bunched them together and were letting them feed right across the road. The wagon rolled closer, but no one seemed in any hurry to move the cows off. Corely hauled back on the reins and stomped down on the brake.

"Damn," he said softly.

"Not again." Mrs. Mattlin straightened tall on the seat, but her words betrayed fear. More than just these cows was bothering her.

"What is it?"

She shifted her view to Corely, eyes wide and lips set in a tight frown. A sharp V cut between her eyebrows. "They just won't leave us alone! Haven't they hurt us enough as it is?"

"It's the Bar JO," Corely said. "Jeb Ollfinger's outfit. They think they own this land."

"This is open range, isn't it?" There might have been two hundred cows milling along the road. Five wranglers were riding a wide circle around them, keeping them together.

Corely snorted. "Try to tell that to Ollfinger. He figured since he come here first he owns it."

Ketcham suddenly understood. He could see Ollfinger's point. A man moves west, fights the land and weather, fights hostile Indians and ruthless outlaws, and builds something for himself. Then sodbusters like the Mattlins come along figuring they're entitled to a piece of it. On the other hand, this was a public road, and it was plain enough Ollfinger's cows were not here by accident. Whatever the right or wrong of the farmers' and the cowmen's land claims, the Mattlins had welcomed Ketcham into their home.

"Just run on through them," he said. "Cows will give way for a wagon and horses."

"Cows might. They won't." Corely jutted his bony chin at three riders making their way toward them.

"How long are they going to keep at us like this?" Mrs. Mattlin's shoulders tensed, and her fists clenched the iron handhold.

"Till they drive us off. That's how long." Corely's words held some of the same despair Ketcham had heard in Mrs. Mattlin's voice.

"Who are they?" The riders were coming across the short-grass prairie at an easy lope.

"Middle one there on the sorrel, his name is Thad Ollfinger. He's old man Ollfinger's son. He's a cocky kid who hides behind his pa's hired help. The fellow to his left, that's Case McGruder. You don't want to go crosswise with him."

Mrs. Mattlin's face tightened, her knuckles beginning to blanch.

The riders were almost upon them, close enough for Ketcham to see the hard set to McGruder's mouth and the sharp-angled face beneath the flat brim of his gray hat. He wore a Colt revolver on his left hip, and rode with his spine ramrod straight and his shoulders thrown back. A big man who thought highly of himself. He'd be a bear in a fight, if appearances were any measure.

25

"And the third?" He shifted around in the box as the riders split to either side of the wagon.

"Wonderly." Mrs. Mattlin spit out the name like poison on her tongue. "His name is Kit Wonderly."

Corely and Ketcham looked at her. Then the riders reined up and circled the wagon.

Wonderly nudged his horse near to Mrs. Mattlin and leaned forward, grinning at her. He was a tall man, nearly Ketcham's own height, or a whisker more, but he didn't pack much meat on his shoulders or chest. Ketcham pegged him to be about twenty-two or-three. He'd had the pox at sometime, and his face had suffered from it. His teeth looked to have taken the brunt of a fist or two. A couple were missing, and those that remained hadn't seen a good scrubbing in a while. A sorry example of a beard gave his face a splotchy red hue. A man who couldn't do any better than that ought to keep a razor handy and use it often.

His view shifted to Thad Ollfinger, the youngest of the three, and not a bad-looking kid. Like McGruder and Wonderly, he wore a gun; right side, a Smith & Wesson, judging by the shape of the grip. He and McGruder had come up on Corely's side of the wagon, but they weren't looking at the old man. They were staring at Ketcham just like he was that wild Comanche in the story, the one who showed up at the ladies' tea party.

"You need to clear them animals off this road," Corely said to McGruder, trying to sound forceful, though his gaze seemed to glance off the man and settle to one side of him.

McGruder's dark eyes moved off of Ketcham and narrowed at Corely. "They're grazing."

"They're blocking the road."

"Not my problem."

Corely winced. "Then . . . then I'm . . . I'm just gonna have to drive through them."

"Might spook 'em. That wouldn't be a smart thing to do." Wonderly's easy reply only thinly masked the threat there.

Thad Ollfinger, grinning like a kitten at a tit, wasn't saying a word but was watching Wonderly with a look of pure admiration.

McGruder's gravelly voice drew Corely's head back around. "Better turn this rig an' go home, Mattlin."

"We have business ahead." Mrs. Mattlin's eyes burned, shifting between them. "You don't own this road."

They were bullies, and they'd found some folks who weren't the fighting sort. Their kind was a vermin and a plague throughout the West, and a man usually didn't have to ride too far before having to deal with one or two of 'em. Ketcham understood that dealing with them in their own way was sometimes the only thing they understood.

27

McGruder's view came back to him. Ketcham returned the stare, unflinching.

Wonderly nudged his horse closer to the wagon. Mrs. Mattlin shifted on the seat away from him. "Mr. Ollfinger considers this his road, seeing as it was his wagons what first cut tracks through this territory."

Maybe he should have kept his mouth shut, but they were pushing pretty hard and Ketcham couldn't see where Corely or Mrs. Mattlin deserved it. "That makes about as much sense as claiming the Oregon Trail belonged to the mountain men because they were the first to put down moccasin track on the land."

The three of them looked at him. "Who are you?" McGruder growled.

His revolver lay just out of reach in the corner of the wagon box. He adjusted his position casually. His and McGruder's eyes locked again. "Just a stranger passing through."

Wonderly snickered. "A stranger sticking his nose in where it don't belong just might get it cut off."

"You think you got it in you to try, boy?" The cool, self-assured edge in Ketcham's voice shaved the grin off Wonderly's face.

Mrs. Mattlin swallowed a short gasp.

He sensed more than saw Corely stiffen, but kept his eyes fixed on the pockfaced fellow. No one said anything for a moment, then Wonderly grinned again. Ketcham grinned too. Out of the corner of his eye McGruder was loosening a lariat and punching a hole in it. They intended to have some fun with him. He got his feet under him, ready. The rope took a swing and opened up. He wasn't there when it hit the box.

Wonderly gave a startled cry as Ketcham drove him off his horse, landing atop him on the far side, slamming the breath from Wonderly's lungs. Hoofbeats started around the wagon. A short jab to the chin put the stunned Wonderly out cold. Leaping to his feet, he yanked Wonderly's carbine from the saddle boot and without breaking stride swung around, laying the barrel hard across McGruder's face.

The man toppled from his saddle.

Coming back around, working the lever, he jacked a shell into the chamber and narrowed an eye over the barrel at the Ollfinger kid.

Thad Ollfinger pulled up hard on his reins and set his horse back on its haunches. He just sat there staring down into the big bore of Wonderly's rifle pointing at his heart.

"One move for that hawgleg, kid, and it'll be your last."

The kid reached for the sky.

"More riders coming, Ketcham." Corely's voice was pitched higher than a mouse's squeak.

"Into the wagon!" Ketcham ordered.

Thad Ollfinger hesitated, staring at the rifle.

"Now!" He didn't have time for the kid to decide, and Thad must have heard the warning in his voice, because the next instant he swung out of the saddle and over the side of the wagon. Ketcham took a step up on a wheel spoke, then into the box right behind the kid. "On your knees."

Thad Ollfinger went down like a penitent before a preacher, and he might have even been praying some, too. Taking a fistful of his shirt-front, Ketcham buried the rifle barrel under the kid's chin and forced his head back with it. "All right, Mr. Mattlin. Take us through those cows."

Two more riders closed in, but seeing him standing there with the boss's kid like that, they backed off a piece and didn't say a word.

"Hope you know what you're getting us in for," Corely groaned.

"Just get us out of here." The wagon lurched and started forward slowly. As he knew they would, the cows moseyed out of the way.

"My pa . . . he ain't goin' to let you get away with this," Thad Ollfinger managed to say with his head cocked back like that.

"Your pa can come see me about it, if he's got a mind to." And as the cows closed in behind them, he had a strong notion that Jeb Ollfinger would be doing just that.

Chapter Three

The sea of cows opened before them, then closed ranks behind them just as the waters had done for Moses and the Hebrew slaves. But Margaret was in no mood to ponder the similarities. Her fist stung at the iron handhold, her knuckles blanching like a dead man's bones. She stared straight ahead as their wagon punched a hole through the herd and out the other side. Corely drove on another few hundred yards before Ketcham told him to stop.

"You head out of here now, boy." When he shifted the rifle from Thad's chin, the kid fled the wagon like a jackrabbit leaving tail fuzz in a coyote's choppers. "And tell your friends to stay clear of us," he called after him. One of the riders loped over and reached to swing the kid up onto his horse behind him.

She knew they wouldn't stay clear, not after what happened, and she suspected Ketcham knew it, too. Had he said that only for her and Corely's sake?

"Ollfinger ain't goin' to sit still for this," Corely warned.

Ketcham grimaced. "Sorry if I made trouble for you."

He must have seen that V that always rested between her eyebrows whenever she was worried. But in spite of her concern, she couldn't hold back a small smile. The Bar JO wranglers deserved being taken down a notch. *Justice?* "They got what they were asking for."

Ketcham gave her a curious look, as if he'd heard something in her voice he approved of.

Corely got the wagon moving at a brisker pace than before, while Ketcham kept an eye on the dust in their wake, holding Kit Wonderly's rifle across his knees.

She straightened around on the seat. She wasn't looking for approval, especially from a drifting man the likes of Chance Ketcham. She just wanted to be left alone so she and Corely could put the broken pieces of their lives back together. That, and justice to be done.

Hank. The memory of her husband came like a peal of thunder out of a cloudless sky—unbidden and unexpected. It was often like that.

They'd made so many plans had so many hopes for building a life together and raising a family. He'd told her the move would be good for them—and she'd believed him. Kansas was settled and fenced, but there was still lots of virgin land in the Territories. Corely had agreed with his son and was eager to make the move, too. She and Dorothy should have said no. Should have stood their ground. Men!

Her fist hardened upon the handhold. She would not cry. She'd shed all the tears she was going to. Her eyes brimmed anyway, and she touched them with the sleeve of her chemisette. "Dust."

Far off to her right, sitting in the middle of nowhere, was the new Grange Hall the farmers had built a little over a year before. The simple square building gleamed like a bright jewel beneath its coat of white paint, looking out of place in the midst of the tawny prairie grass. She remembered the first social they had there, and how families from twenty miles around came to christen the new building. There'd been a band and music and dancing. A long table overflowed with meats and cakes and vegetables, and in the center had been two bowls of punch, one hard and the other soft.

Some of the local cowboys had dropped in too, and they'd been welcomed to join the festivities. Mostly they were young men, curious about what the farmers were up to now. Perhaps some were eyeing the activities and reporting back to the big ranches like Ollfinger's Bar JO, or McCormick's Tumble T outfit.

Kit Wonderly had been there. She remembered how he'd swaggered in with his partners and stood looking the place over. Though not particularly eye-pleasing, he had a way of walking that caught a woman's eye. She'd wondered about this man with the big spurs and wide hat. He looked dangerous, and sort of dashing in his tight vest, wearing a six-shooter on his hip—the kind of fantasy man a woman might fashion in a moment of whimsy to dress up a corn-shuck and chapped-hands life.

She'd meant nothing with her innocent flirtations. She was a married woman, and she loved her husband. How could she know what sort of man Kit Wonderly really was . . . or his friends?

He'd made straight for the punch bowl and spent the first hour not straying far from it. He'd seen her watching, reading more into it than was there.

It was all her fault. How could she have seen the end of saying yes when he'd asked her to dance? Why did dangerous men catch her eye? After the music stopped she'd fled back to the safety of Hank's side, shaking from the vile words Wonderly had whispered near her ear. But she never told Hank. The last thing she wanted was for Hank to make a scene right there. It was supposed to be a festive time!

A small shudder brought her view back into focus. The Grange Hall was far behind them. She put her eyes on the road ahead and another lone white building, this one with a steeple pointed skyward.

Corely turned the team off the main road onto a pair of ruts and drew up in front of the church. The Johnsons' black buggy stood nearby, a leggy chestnut still in its traces nipping the sparse brown grass in the shade alongside the building.

"Pastor and Susan are here," she noted.

Corely set the brake, and Ketcham jumped over the side to help her down.

"We'll only be a minute," Corely told Ketcham.

She gathered up her bundle of flowers and they started toward the back of the church.

Ketcham cast another look over his shoulder. There was still no sign of McGruder and the others. He strolled into the shade of the clapboard building and rolled a cigarette, drawing the smoke into his lungs and relaxing against a corner of the church. Out back was a cemetery, corralled behind a low, iron fence. Corely and Mrs. Mattlin stood over two headstones, their heads bowed. He watched them, curious, but not wanting to intrude. Was her husband in one of those graves? Corely's narrow shoulders gave a small shudder, and he leaned closer and spoke something to her. She nodded, divided her flowers,

35

and stooped to place some on each of the graves.

"Good morning, mister," said a deep voice from somewhere behind him. Ketcham turned and lifted his chin toward the big man standing in the open door. He wore black trousers and a white shirt unbuttoned at the throat. He was hatless, and his skin was sunburned. A full salt-and-pepper beard encircled his face. Blue eyes were set deep below bushy eyebrows black as coal, the same color as the thick mop of hair atop his broad head. His arms were massive. His fists, wrapped around the handle of a broom, made it appear spindly. He stood there looking Ketcham up and down, then smiled suddenly. "The morning is warming up, stranger. I've got a crock of cool water inside."

"I could use something to cut the dust."

He spied the wagon. "The Mattlins here?"

Ketcham hooked a thumb over his shoulder.

"Ah." Understanding briefly saddened his eyes. "You a friend of Corely and Margaret?"

"Just met yesterday. I needed a place to sleep, and he had a barn that wasn't being used."

"That would be his way. Corely's not a man to turn away a stranger in need. 'Be not forgetful to entertain strangers: for thereby some have entertained angels unawares.' "

Ketcham thought that a queer thing for a grown man to say. He stared at him, trying to sort out what he'd meant by it. "I sure ain't no angel."

The tall man gave a friendly laugh that began deep down in his chest and rumbled up like thunder through a canyon. "None of us are." He nodded for Ketcham to follow.

Crushing the cigarette underfoot and doffing his hat, he entered the little church. There were only two rows of pews inside the narrow building, and altogether, maybe fifty folks could have crowded into the place at one time, and that would have made for a right tucked-up Sunday morning. Three windows on each side let in light. Even with the side door open and all the windows up, and a faint breeze moving through the place, it was oven hot and smelled of clay dust. Up at the front there was no cross like he'd come to expect, only a simple raised pulpit, a piano to one side, and an American flag on a short pole in the east corner. In the west corner a door stood open to a small room, and as they stepped inside, a woman's face peered curiously out.

It was an attractive face, crossed here and there with stray strands of brown hair that had worked themselves loose from the pins. She wore a simple gray dress. The shaft of a mop was in her hand.

"My wife, Susan," he said.

"Chance Ketcham, ma'am."

"Welcome to our church, Mr. Ketcham." She smiled.

"I'm Reverend Johnson. Liam Johnson." The preacher man had a bone-crushing grip. He stepped to the pulpit, where a crockery jug and ladle sat, and dipped out water into a tin cup. It was sweet and cold, as if just raised from a well. "Mr. Ketcham is a friend of the Mattlins."

"Are they here?"

"Out back . . . visiting."

Susan set the mop aside, tucked her hair back in place, and brushed at her dress. "I'll just be a few minutes, Liam."

He nodded as she went outside. The two men stood there awhile, not speaking. Reverend Johnson was the first to break the silence. "Hot weather."

Ketcham peered out a window. "Usual for this time of year. That grass could use some rain."

"It will come. It always does."

"Who's buried out back in the boneyard?"

"Corely's wife, and his son."

Mrs. Mattlin's husband. So he'd been right. Johnson took a cup of water for himself. "You're not from around these parts, are you, Mr. Ketcham?"

He gave Reverend Johnson the same story he'd given the Mattlins. The silence crept back.

"Who is this fellow, Jeb Ollfinger?" Ketcham thought he knew most of the ranchers in West Texas and the eastern New Mexico Territory. This place wasn't so far off that he shouldn't have heard of the outfits around.

"Ollfinger?" A scowl darkened the preacher's

38

face. "Why you asking? You didn't have trouble with him?"

"His cows were blocking the road."

"Hmmm." He nodded.

"So I decided to move 'em." Ketcham grinned. "Afraid I made myself right unpopular among some of his hands. Was wondering what the Mattlins might be up against."

Johnson smiled and let a low laugh rumble out. "You just moved, then, huh?" He sipped some water from the cup, which seemed tiny in his hands. "Jeb Ollfinger came out here about twenty years ago, shortly after the War. He's not a bad sort once you get to know him, but he doesn't like farmers, and he gives his hired hands a free rein with them." He shook his head. "Sometimes I wonder if Jeb really knows all that goes on. He's got a rough bunch riding for him. He owns about twenty thousand acres, but he claims rights to a lot more. He runs about five, six hundred head come a good year."

"Sounds pretty small-time."

Johnson shrugged. "To some folks, maybe. He doesn't consider himself small-time."

"The Bar JO would fit into a corner of one of Charlie Goodnight's pastures."

Johnson laughed again and nodded knowingly. "Well, for being small-time, he sure makes a lot of big-time trouble." He frowned suddenly. "If you go crossways with Jeb Ollfinger, you could be in for a hard time of it. He doesn't back off easy. Oh, there was a time when Jeb was most amiable, but ever since the farmers began filling up the land, he's become uncompromising. I think he wants to show folks around here he still holds an iron grip on the land. That if he lets up even once, he's going to lose it all. He's in a war he can't win, but too headstrong, or maybe too fearful, to admit it. Times are changing, Mr. Ketcham. Statehood is almost certain—if not this year or next, certainly in Jeb's lifetime."

"Land disputes are exactly what will hold up statehood."

"I know that. And the Territorial governor in Santa Fe is trying to sort out the rat's nest of claims and Spanish land grants right now. Eventually it will happen, and when it does, and there is statehood, there will be no stopping folks from putting up fences and taking legal deeds to most of this land he runs his cows on now. If Jeb Ollfinger is ever to keep control of the land, he has to make his stand now, not later."

The reverend was right, but Ketcham couldn't see where he could fault Mr. Ollfinger too much. He was here first, and to Ketcham's way of thinking that sort of gave him prior rights. The right or wrong of it aside, the middle of a land dispute is not where he wanted to be. "In the meantime, what law is there in Carson or any of these other little towns?"

"Not much. There's a federal marshal who makes his way through here occasionally, and another one west of here in Lincoln County. Other than that, people handle trouble any way they can." He frowned. "And that usually means someone ends up shot or swinging."

"So folks like the Mattlins put up fences and men like Jeb Ollfinger herd their cows onto public roads."

Johnson rolled his powerful shoulders. "I don't like it either, but that's about the way it is."

They heard voices coming toward the church. Mrs. Mattlin, Corely, and Mrs. Johnson stepped inside.

"I see you already met our preacher," Corely said.

"Mr. Ketcham and me, we've been having us a good talk, Corely." Reverend Johnson took Corely's hand in his bear paw and gave it a hearty shake.

Susan Johnson said, "Margaret has been telling me about what happened on the road. I'm just so thankful no one was hurt."

"That McGruder fellow will be hurting some," Corely allowed, and frowned.

"What did happen?" Reverend Johnson looked at Ketcham like he'd not told the whole story.

Mrs. Johnson plunged into a detailed account of the incident as she'd gotten it from Mrs. Mattlin, only she embellished and polished it way more than necessary. She spoke quickly, and moved her hands in big circles and short jabs,

41

and Ketcham could see she was infected with Mr. Ned Buntline's affliction for spinning a yarn. When she finished, her husband only shook his head, then looked at Ketcham. "Jeb Ollfinger isn't going to like it when he hears. Especially the way you handled his boy."

"I'll try to stay out of his way."

The Johnsons and Mattlins spent a few minutes talking about crops, and about someone in the congregation named Conner who'd taken ill with the gout, and a woman named Betia expecting a baby. Ketcham was again the outsider. Then they all said good-bye and promised to see each other come Sunday morning. By the time he and the Mattlins climbed back into the wagon, a better part of the morning was behind them.

The little town of Carson was only up the road. Ketcham had hardly settled in place when the hot air telegraphed the odor of fresh manure. He hitched himself up. The building on his left was the livery. Beyond it stood about eight or nine other structures, all strung out loosely along either side of the road. Somewhere, someone was driving nails with a regular cadence. Maybe a dozen or so houses sat back off a narrow side street. Along the main street a few horses nosed the hitching rails, batting away flies with lazy tails. A wagon rolled past them, its harness chains jingling softly. Corely gave the driver a friendly wave, then turned down a dirt track and parked alongside a general mercantile store.

42

"You are welcome to join us, Mr. Ketcham, if you like," Mrs. Mattlin said. "Just have some shopping to do, a few items to pick up at the hardware store. But we'll likely be gone for a while."

"Thanks, ma'am, but you and your father-in-law do what you have to. I'll just hang around the wagon here in the shade where its cool."

"Might be a few hours," Corely said, adjusting feedbags upon the horses. He grinned. "Got some visiting to catch up on. We don't make it into town but two or three times a month."

"I'll be all right. Haven't got any money to spend anyhow." He'd left his poke back in his saddlebags in the barn.

Corely and Mrs. Mattlin went on their way. He studied the dusty track and the clapboard buildings. Carson wasn't much—like the dozens of other places he'd passed through since leaving his parents' home. This dry land was a world away from where he'd grown up. Back in Arkansas were lakes and creeks, and rivers worthy of the name. Here, any little trickle down a dusty rill might be called a river, and if there was enough water to take a bath in, it'd be a lake sure enough. He grinned. Even a dirt stock tank sometimes got saddled with that handle.

His thoughts returned to that church, and of Corely and Mrs. Mattlin standing over those graves. Neither one of them had mentioned them.

"Did I hear you say you hadn't got two pennies to rub together?"

He looked over at a short, plump man in black trousers, a white shirt, and a black vest, leaning against the doorjamb to the general store, a cane in his right hand. He didn't look old enough to be needing a walking stick, but by the way he stood there, hunched over, it was plain he'd gotten himself stoved up real bad.

"Not much to speak of, and none in my pockets as of now."

"You look to be a strapping fellow. Got a wagon out back that needs unloading. I'd do it myself, except I fell and busted a rib and knocked my knee out of place last week doing a fandango with a butter churn. There's four bits in it for you if you want the job. Won't take you but an hour at most."

"Four bits?"

"All I can offer."

Ketcham had nothing better to do than stand around holding up the side of the wall with his shoulder. He grinned. "Show me where it is."

Chapter Four

Horace Hawkins kept out of his way, directing with that cane of his where this box was to go or that crate was to be stacked. Ketcham hefted and hauled, shoved and adjusted, and about forty-five minutes later had everything out of the wagon and placed where Hawkins could finish the job.

In that three quarters of an hour he'd learned that Hawkins had come from Illinois about five years before, that this one-horse town of Carson was barely holding its own and if it didn't start growing he'd have to pull up stakes and move on farther west. He lamented not having set up business in Riley's Switch, where at least there was a railroad.

Ketcham had seen Riley's Switch and wondered how anyone could want to settle there.

Hawkins went on to speculate on California, but figured it was a long piece off and reckoned he'd likely find someplace along the way to suit him.

"It's the farmers and the ranchers," he said at one point. "Until they settle their differences, this town is doomed."

"All the ranchers?"

"Well," Hawkins pushed out a thick lower lip and thought it over some. "Mostly it's Jeb Ollfinger. But the other cowmen will back him if push comes to shove. None want the farmers fencing off open range."

"Can't say as I blame 'em."

He shrugged. "Me, I try to stay out of it. I sell to both cowmen and sodbusters."

"Someday you might have to pick sides."

Hawkins gave a small smile, his pink cheeks puffing out. "The day I have to choose sides, that's the day I close up shop and drive out of here."

"California?"

"Who knows."

Hawkins paid Ketcham fifty cents and thanked him for the help. A few minutes later Ketcham found himself on the boardwalk outside Hawkins's door, suddenly feeling mighty thirsty. Casting his eyes about, he spied the local watering hole up the street, tucked between a gun-

smith's shop and a harness maker. With a grin
and a flick of his thumb, he snatched the coin out
of the air, shoved it into his pocket, and bent his
steps toward the One Stop Saloon.

"What will it be, stranger?" a wiry fellow in a
dingy apron asked when he stepped up to the
painted plank that served as a bar. The saloon
looked narrow enough to spit across. There was
only room enough for a single row of six tables
hard against the wall. At the rear of the building
was a closed door that probably opened into a
storeroom out back. All in all, the One Stop Saloon was a hole-in-the-wall, but it was a hole doing a brisk business. Five gents bellied into the
bar, sipping beers or whiskey. Four of the six
tables were occupied.

"Beer," he told the barkeep. He slapped the
fifty-cent piece onto the bar and got his drink and
forty-five cents in change. The far table was un-
occupied and he made for it, settled into a chair,
and leaned back until the chair bumped the wall
behind him. He took a sip and found the beer to
be warm. Well, he hadn't expected it to be icy
cold. That was surely more than a man could
hope for in a two-bit saloon like this. But it was
tasty, and he'd drunk worse.

Across the narrow room, past all the hats and
faces, a bright rectangle of sunlight fell through
the open front door and partway into the saloon.
Dust motes glinted in the shaft of light, and under its glare the worn floorboards showed wide

gaps where they had hastily been nailed in place.

A clock on the wall behind the bar ticked loudly enough to be heard above the murmur of men's voices. Ketcham noted the time, figuring he'd give the Mattlins another hour to finish up with their shopping and socializing. He had forty-five cents in his pocket, and at a nickel a throw, if he was diligent, he might work his way clear through another twenty cents' worth of beers in that time.

He was feeling relaxed, but a part of him remained alert. Somewhere right now McGruder, and young Ollfinger, and that third fellow, Wonderly, would be making plans for revenge. There was no doubt they'd be thinking of such things, for that's how men like those three saw life. They might even show up here in Carson. Ketcham had no desire to get between the farmers and ranchers again.

He recalled how Mrs. Mattlin had acted near Wonderly. Wonderly was interested in her, it was plain. And it was just as plain she wanted nothing to do with him. Sensible woman, that one. Ketcham grinned into his beer mug.

He glanced out the window to where the Mattlins' wagon stood empty across the street. He could see it plainly from where he sat. His gaze returned to the men in the saloon. Cowboys mostly, from the looks of them. As he looked around the room, his eyes were suddenly drawn back to the window.

Six men came into view, riding slowly past the Mattlins' wagon. Upon seeing it, they reined in and spoke among themselves. Wonderly was among them.

Ketcham put down his beer and went to the door. At the moment the rider's attention was on Hawkins's store. Ketcham slipped outside and moved into the narrow gap of deep shadow between the saloon and the harness shop. An older man seemed to be in charge. The Ollfinger kid was among them. McGruder wasn't there. Ketcham wasn't surprised. McGruder would be nursing a mighty sore face about now, and maybe a broken jaw. He'd hit him pretty hard.

They sat there awhile, talking and peering up and down the street. One of the men dismounted and went inside the general mercantile store and came back a few minutes later shaking his head. The old man waved an arm and the men split off in different directions, as men do when looking for something . . . or someone.

Ketcham slipped out from between the buildings and inside the harness shop. A pair of saddlebags lay on a table by the window, and he pretended to be interested in them. The shop proprietor tried to be helpful, but Ketcham told him he was only shopping and not ready to buy anything yet. Past the plate-glass window, young Ollfinger and the old man rode up the street. There was a family resemblance.

"Is that Jeb Ollfinger?"

The proprietor, anxious to turn a dollar, glanced out the window and nodded. "That's him."

Ollfinger looked to be about sixty, still solidly built but with a bit of a paunch beginning to creep over his belt buckle. His face was nut brown from the sun and weathered like old wood, and what Ketcham could see of the fringes of his hair was about the same color as the gray Stetson he wore. Ketcham started for the door.

"I'll give you a good price on those bags."

"Some other time."

The men were nearing the opposite sides of town, their backs to him. Ketcham dipped his head and made for the mercantile store. Horace Hawkins seemed surprised to see him again.

"Spend it already?"

"Only a nickel. How much for a box of forty-fours?" He had a box of shells in his saddlebags back in the barn at the Mattlins' place, but if there was going to be trouble here they were no use to him, and he wanted more than the five rounds he carried in his revolver.

"Seventy-five cents."

"What would I have to do to earn another thirty cents?"

Hawkins's fleshy face brightened and lengthened out into a smile. "I thought it might be you they were looking for."

Ketcham tried not to let his concern show. "What did you tell 'em?"

"Told Aug Honniger I hadn't seen the Mattlins. Didn't say nothing about you."

"Honniger? He the one who came in here?"

"You've got a good eye, mister."

"Why didn't you tell them about me?"

"Like I said, I don't come between the cowmen and the farmers." His eyes narrowed. "Although you don't look much like a farmer. But the Mattlins are good folk. That's why I didn't tell them." He paused, working his thick lips as he thought. "I can discount a box of forty-fours. How does forty-five cents sound?"

Ketcham dug the money from his pocket and took the weighty box of cartridges.

"Hope you won't be needing those." Hawkins thumped the coins into his cash register.

"Me too." He filled the empty loops in his gunbelt, crushed down the box some, and shoved what remained into his pocket. Out on the main street some of the Bar JO men had come together again. He had a nervous feeling for the Mattlins, even though it was probably him Jeb Ollfinger wanted to get his fingers into.

"The Mattlins said they were going to visit someone. You wouldn't know their friends?"

Hawkins shrugged. "Could be most anybody. I don't keep track of people's comings and goings."

Ketcham told himself they'd be all right and glanced out the window again. There were only four riders on the street now. Where had the other two gotten off to? "I need to use your back door?"

"You know where it is."

He cut through the storeroom and out onto a weedy dirt track behind the streetfront buildings. A few horses, a buggy, and a couple wagons were parked here, but otherwise it was deserted. Across the lane to his right was the back side of a solitary building facing the side street. A few scattered houses stood some distance away. The Mattlins could be anywhere.

He started off to his left, but the sudden clatter of a board hitting the ground pulled him up short and he hunkered down behind a wagon. Those two missing men saved him the trouble of having to find them. They stuck their heads around a corner two buildings down, then came out onto the track he'd been following a moment before. One was the fellow who'd gone into Hawkins's place to inquire of the Mattlins. Aug Honniger, Hawkins had called him. Honniger pointed at a distant house, and the other shook his head. They talked a moment, then split, Honniger heading straight toward the wagon Ketcham was behind.

As Honniger drew near, Ketcham's fists bunched. His legs went taut like a spring, ready to take him low and hard and put him down fast.

"Hey, Augie."

Honniger swung around. His partner waved him back.

Ketcham let go of a breath and relaxed against the wagon's wheel hub. At the far end of the alley the two men talked a few seconds, then started toward the main street. He hurried down the gap next to Hawkins's store. Out front the men regrouped and mounted up. Ollfinger, straight in his saddle and unsmiling, glanced along the main street one last time, then nodded as if coming to a decision and started out of town. His men lined out behind him. They rounded a bend and disappeared behind the livery.

"Find your friends?" Hawkins asked when Ketcham closed the door behind him.

"No, and neither did Ollfinger."

"Don't know what you all did to cross him—an' I don't want to know. Only hope you can work it out before someone gets hurt."

"Might be too late for that."

Hawkins frowned, then took up his cane and busied himself arranging cans on a shelf.

"Where is the Bar JO?"

"About five miles west of here. If you came by way of the Mattlins' farm you went right past the cutoff—a half a mile or so before you come to the church."

That would have put the cutoff about where Ollfinger had parked his cows on the road.

Hawkins glanced over and pursed his lips. "Just what is it you're fixing on doing, mister?"

"I thought you didn't get involved?"

He frowned and went back to arranging cans.

Corely and Mrs. Mattlin came across the street. They stepped up onto the boardwalk and the door opened.

Corely didn't seem surprised to see Ketcham there. "Did you see 'em? They come a-looking for us just like I knew they would."

Margaret clutched her handbag in both fists. Mrs. Mattlin's worry had obviously increased. "Are you all right?"

He nodded. "It's me they're after." He was causing the Mattlins more trouble. For their sakes, it was time to be moving on.

"It's all of us." Corely hunched his narrow shoulders and stared out the window.

"We have as much right to be here as they do." Mrs. Mattlin's eyebrows pinched in that sharp V again.

"It'll blow over." Ketcham tried to sound re-assuring, but she wasn't having any of it. Plainly, Mrs. Mattlin wasn't a woman who sugarcoated her troubles.

"They scoured the town looking for us. We were visiting Emma Dietz. Luckily we saw them coming and stayed in Emma's house."

Corely gave her hand a reassuring pat. "We'll straighten it out."

"It will end up like last time." Her words were strained, with a catch in her voice, and Ketcham realized this might go just a tad deeper than he'd thought.

"No, no, we won't let it come to that." Corely chewed his lips.

Almost as if wanting to put an end to that line of thought, Hawkins's cane tapped the floor and he came a couple steps closer. "Your order came in the other day, Corely. I've got it in the back room."

With a sigh and a shake of his head, Corely picked up on Hawkins's cue. "Mind giving me a hand, Mr. Ketcham?"

Ketcham was anxious to cut the tension too, and trailed after them into the back storeroom. Hawkins pointed to four spools of barbed wire sitting off to one side. Ketcham frowned, but kept his feelings to himself and helped carry the spools around to the wagon alongside the store, then loaded them aboard. Corely removed the feedbags from his horses and tossed them into the wagon as they waited while Mrs. Mattlin paid Hawkins.

Mrs. Mattlin came out of the store and climbed angrily up onto the seat before Ketcham could reach her to help her up. She tucked a brown-paper bundle under the seat and straightened around. "Let's get home."

Ketcham swung into the wagon box and settled down in the corner. Corely clucked his animals ahead and drove them out of town.

Chapter Five

Ketcham kept one eye peeled for Ollfinger and his wranglers all the way back to the Mattlins' farm. Corely and Mrs. Mattlin were looking over their shoulders too, and he reckoned they were thinking the open prairie might be a good place for Ollfinger to deal with them. His six-shooter rode unthonged in his holster, and Wonderly's rifle was within reach, but the ride turned out to be uneventful. Just the same, no one said much more than five words the whole way, and everyone seemed to take in a breath and relax when Corely turned the team onto the road to his place.

He pulled to a halt in front of the house and stabbed a foot to the brake while Mrs. Mattlin

56

climbed down and took her package inside. They rolled on to the barn, where he helped Corely unhitch the horses and put them up in the corral.

Ketcham retrieved a brush from a pail and started down the withers of one of his scrawny beasts. "You know Ollfinger. What's he likely to do?"

Corely glanced at the house, a frown pulling at his face. "He's not a man to let what you done go by."

"If I'm gone, maybe he won't bother you and Mrs. Mattlin?"

"He was doing that before you showed up." Corely levered one of the horses' hind legs onto his knee, examined the hoof, and worked at a stone with a pick. He plucked it out, cleaned the frog, then dropped the hoof, straightening up slowly with a hand pressed to the small of his back, giving a low grunt. "You didn't light no new fire under him, Mr. Ketcham. Only fed the flames some."

He'd figured it that way. Just the same, he knew he should be moving again. Him being away from there would be one less reason for Ollfinger's boys to give the Mattlins a rough time. "Show me the wood you want cut."

Corely moved stiffly as he took Ketcham into the stand of cottonwoods. Just as he'd suspected, there was a seep among the trees. In places the moist ground was springy beneath his feet. Sometime in the past, someone had felled five or six good-size trees. They were long dead and dry, and lay about at the far edge of the grove. Beyond was another field Corely had begun working. It was partly furrowed but did not appear to have ever been planted, although it was a good deal greener than the rest of the land around it. He wondered what kind of grass could be so bright in this dry land.

His lips tightened. A man had to put in an awful lot of backbreaking work to grow sweet potatoes in this harsh country. He remembered the work his father put into their little farm in Arkansas, and that was favorable land for farming. He wanted none of that for himself. This new field had apparently sat fallow since the ground had first been broken. Maybe that's why it looked so fresh and bright. What made Corely abandon it after putting so much work into it?

"You can start on those. The wood is seasoned and it cuts easy. Got an ax and a bucksaw in the toolshed, and a sharpening wheel in the barn."

He followed Corely to the toolshed, collected the tools, and spent fifteen minutes pumping the sharpening wheel and honing a new edge to the ax. The saw frame was big enough for two men to handle, but one could make out with it all right. He carried the tools back to the trees.

He'd cut a heap of wood in his day, and he leaned his rifle against a tree, stripped off his shirt, and set to work on those downed trees like there was no tomorrow. Partly he just enjoyed the work, but partly it was because once he'd turned out two cords, his obligation to the Mattlins would be fulfilled and he could be on his way.

He put in about two hours' work with the bucksaw and had prepared about a dozen rounds to split when he finally set the saw aside and reached for the ax. Setting one of the smaller pieces on end atop the largest round, he halved it in a single stroke, righted the pieces, and halved them again. It was tiring work, but his muscles hadn't begun to complain yet. He quartered two more rounds in short order. The sweat was slick upon his back and the evening breeze cooled his skin.

All at once the hairs at the back of his neck rose. He came down hard with the ax, buried it in a log, and snatched up his Winchester, thumbing back the hammer as he swung around, crouched low.

Mrs. Mattlin jumped, her eyes big and staring, the water in the glass she was holding sloshing a little over the rim.

He let go of a breath and tilted the barrel away from her. "Sorry, ma'am. Didn't mean to startle you."

She gulped and started to breathe again. She had changed out of her earlier clothes into a plain brown dress. It was nothing fancy, but somehow it suited her.

59

"Best if you call out before coming up behind someone like that." A woman living in the country should know that much.

"I'm . . . I didn't know." She stared at the rifle.

He leaned it back against the tree. "Is that for me?"

She seemed to have forgotten the glass in her hand. She looked at it, then nodded. "Are you always so nervous, Mr. Ketcham?"

"It doesn't pay to be careless. And today's been some eventful."

She scowled and handed him the water. Disapproval again?

"Thanks." The water was cold, and he drank the glass dry.

"So how long have you been hauling freight, Mr. Ketcham?"

He caught her tone. Mrs. Mattlin was a shrewd woman, and he couldn't see where he could keep on lying.

"Not very long."

"I didn't think so."

It was strange the way her disapproval stole the wind from his sails. Why hadn't he just spoken the truth from the start? "Fact is, ma'am, I've not hauled freight but maybe two or three times in my life, and that was some years ago."

"Then why did you feel the need to lie to us?"

"It wasn't a lie . . . not exactly, ma'am. Like I said, I've done some hauling—"

"But you deliberately misled us."

60

He grimaced. "I guess that's mostly true."

"Why?"

"Well, you and Corely are farmers, and I'm a cowman, and I was darned tired."

Her expression, if not exactly softening, at least didn't harden. "If you're a cowman, why did you take our part against Ollfinger?"

"I don't cotton to bullies, ma'am. And I was indebted to you for your hospitality."

Some of the fire left her eyes. "That wouldn't matter to some men." She searched his face and started to say something else, but stopped herself. "It couldn't be that you were brought here for a reason?"

"A reason?"

"Maybe you're meant to . . . to help us?"

Now he understood. He expelled a hard breath. "I don't know where you got that notion. I'm not the sort of man God would send to see to your troubles." And the sooner he was on his way, the better.

"Are you on the run?"

"From the law? No."

"Then what?"

He glanced at the glass and handed it back to her. "Let's just say I got crossways with some fellows back in Bailey. I'd walked away from a poker table with more of their money than they cared to give up, so they came beating the bushes for my hide. I had no good reason to hang around

61

Bailey anyway, so I packed my saddlebags and moved on."

"You do that often? Pack your saddlebags and move on?"

"It's easier that way. Besides, I generally figure there's always something better over the next hill." He grinned at her. Darn, she was a hard woman to get a smile out of.

"Did you cheat?"

"Cheat?" Ketcham gave a short laugh. "Didn't have to. They were playing reckless. They'd more to drink than they should have—and so did I, but my head was clearer, I suppose, and I just kept taking their money until I seen it was time to back out of the game. Gellerman, he was getting nervous with his losing, and he's a dangerous man when he gets nervous."

"Gellerman?" Her eyes compressed suddenly.

What had he said now? "Benny Gellerman. A wrangler over at the Muleshoe outfit. I worked for the outfit awhile, but I was getting itchy feet again. It was time for me to move on. Gellerman was the nudge I needed."

She eyed him warily. Did she not believe him? Or maybe she was only trying to sort through all he had told her. Either way, her sudden eagerness dimmed.

"And now what?" Her low voice was cautious, and although she hadn't moved a single step, something had driven a wedge between them. And like a fool, he wanted it out.

He took a step closer. "I don't know yet. Figured I'll move on. This land is getting too filled up for my liking." So why was he standing there looking at this woman whose troubles were not his own?

"And where could you go where it's not filling up? The whole country is growing . . . filling up." She was a practical woman, and wouldn't go pulling up roots and moving on a whim. Not that he had ever put down roots very deep. He had torn his up when he'd left his parents' farm back in Arkansas twelve years earlier. He'd never given them much of a chance to take hold since.

"There must be someplace." And now that distance between them wasn't enough.

Her tone took on an icy quality. "We thought so too." She frowned at the glass in her hand and her shoulders gave a small heave. "But all we did was exchange one trouble for another. Hank and Corely, they both said the grass would be greener out here in the Territories."

Hank must have been her husband. Ketcham didn't remember her mentioning him before.

"So we sold everything we had in Kansas, left family and friends, bought this old farm, and poured our hearts and souls into it." She gave a brittle laugh. "No one bothered to tell us that Ollfinger had driven the former owners off like he's trying to do us."

She gave him a sudden, piercing look. "The only place the grass is really ever greener is atop a grave, Mr. Ketcham." Bitterness edged her words and darkened her face.

He wanted to run for the hills.

She drew in a ragged breath and let it out. "Dinner will be in half an hour. It will be almost dark by then, and you'll be wanting to quit here for the day."

"Thank you, ma'am."

She walked back to the house, but he remained standing there long after she'd gone inside. What she wanted came nowhere near his plans. He wasn't some savior sent to end their troubles. Far from it! So she *had* pulled up roots after all.

He took up the ax and went back to work. He wasn't like some men who could sort through a problem sitting down. Her words might be true about no place being better than another, but he didn't want to believe that. It was time to get moving. He didn't want to put down his roots again—especially not here.

Chapter Six

He got back to the woodpile early the next day, working the saw with a vengeance and swinging the ax until his muscles burned. He'd laid in about a cord of wood by the time he set the big log splitter aside and sat back against a tree, his arms limp upon his knees, his head drooped. He was breathing hard and was slicker than a Kentucky thoroughbred crossing the finish line. He had no notion of how much time had passed, but judging by the lay of the shadows, he reckoned it was nigh onto the noon hour. The pump across the way looked inviting, but there was just no strength left in him, so he sat there expanding his lungs and watching the sweat from his forehead make wet spots upon the dust between his boots.

The sound of approaching horses snapped his head up. Four riders loped up the lane and drew rein in the yard. Jeb Ollfinger, Wonderly, and McGruder. He didn't recognize the fourth man. Ollfinger called to the house. The door opened, and Corely stepped out.

Even at a distance, the bruise on McGruder's face was plain. Ketcham couldn't hear their words. He grabbed up the rifle and worked his way through the trees. The grove thinned out toward the house, but by that time he was already behind the house, out of sight. In a sprint, he reached the back wall, then worked along the side to a place where he could hear.

"I've been patient with you so far, Mattlin," Jeb Ollfinger was saying, "but when your hired hand starts making trouble, then the time's come for me to step in."

"Make trouble?" Corely said. "Why, if that ain't the pot calling the kettle black! It's been you and your boys what's been making trouble since the day we moved in here."

"Moving here was your first mistake."

"No, sir. It was your mistake, Ollfinger. You could have bought this place fair and honest jest like we done. But you didn't. You figured because you'd used the land first, it was yours to take. Well, that ain't so no more, and I got legal

66

papers to prove it. Now, you're trespassing and I'm tellin' you to get off my place."

McGruder nosed his horse into the porch rail. "Where's the sonuvabitch?"

"I ain't got no hired hands here. Couldn't afford 'em if I wanted to. You murdered the only help I ever had." Corely's voice quavered.

Ollfinger stiffened. "A man shouldn't make accusations with no proof."

McGruder broke in again. "Where is he? I owe him."

"You mean Ketcham? I don't know. He ain't a hired hand. Just a man passing through."

McGruder shot a glance around the place, then back at Corely. "You're hiding him."

Ketcham had heard enough and stepped around the corner. Their hands moved for their guns. His Winchester came up. They eased back, and he figured their mamas had taught them manners where guns were concerned.

"You want me, McGruder?"

"I want a piece of you, all right."

Ketcham looked at each of them. Ollfinger was scowling, his dark eyes smoky and full of anger. Did he really believe Corely had picked a fight out on the road? Wonderly was grinning like he was looking forward to what was coming next. The unknown man, with sandy hair and needing a shave, made no sign one way or the other. It wasn't his fight, this rancher-farmer feud, and he didn't appear inclined to get any more involved than what he had to, to keep his boss happy. McGruder, however, radiated pure hate. He'd been bested by Ketcham in front of men who respected him—or at least feared him. He'd lost something in that, and he intended to win it back today.

Ketcham's eyes steadied on the red and purple bruise that marked one side of McGruder's face. "You want me? Climb down off that horse, then." He handed Corely the rifle. "I'll count on you to keep 'em honest whilst I tend to this matter."

Corely took the rifle with some uncertainty. Mrs. Mattlin stepped out of the house, stopping beside him. Her worried eyes darted from the Bar JO men to Ketcham and back.

Ollfinger's stormy gaze never wavered. He'd taken a two-handed grasp upon the pommel of his saddle, sitting there stiff and unyielding like Ketcham had seen him back in Carson. "So you're the one who whipped my men and threatened my son?"

Up close, Ollfinger's face showed the ravages of both age and a life lived hard in a hard land. Ketcham couldn't quite make out the color of his eyes.

"I only finished what your boys started, Ollfinger. And the way I remember it, I went gentle with your son."

"According to my men, you're the one who started it."

"Then you weren't given the straight of it. Your men blocked off a public road with cattle wearing your brand. That looked to me like they were starting it."

Ollfinger cast a quick glance at McGruder, then back at Ketcham. "My men had orders not to make trouble."

"Your men don't follow orders too well."

Ollfinger's scowl darkened with a fierce anger roiling behind his narrowed eyes. Ketcham couldn't tell if that anger was directed at him or at McGruder. Ollfinger was an old man now, but in his day would have been one tough hombre—maybe he still was. But Ollfinger wasn't his immediate problem.

McGruder was a big man. Although Ketcham was no lightweight himself, McGruder had an inch or two and maybe thirty pounds on him. McGruder swung off his saddle, a smile of anticipation creasing his bruised face. But as his boots hit the ground, he winced. Trying not to let the pain show, he casually unbuckled his gunbelt and slung it over the saddle horn.

As they moved away from the horses it was plain McGruder was hurting. He would try to protect his swollen face at first. To do so meant he'd have to hold back some. Ketcham intended to use that to his advantage.

Circling, knuckles bunched and hard, McGruder lunged first. Ketcham easily dodged left, his fist striking out, skimming McGruder's chin.

69

McGruder dodged and ducked for a low jab. Instead of backing away from him as would be natural, Ketcham twisted sideways, bringing him in close enough to land a solid blow to McGruder's jaw.

McGruder staggered, clutching his face. The pain momentarily startled him, then a fire raged in his eyes and he ducked his head and came on like a charging bull. He hit Ketcham hard, knocking the wind out of him as they both crashed to the ground. Ketcham tore free of McGruder's grasp and was back on his feet like a dropped cat. So was McGruder. They went around some more, keeping their distance, glaring at each other.

All at once, McGruder flung a handful of dirt that he must have taken up while on the ground. Ketcham shut his eyes and turned his head. The breeze at his back scattered most of the dust, but it gave McGruder a momentary edge and he raged in, fists like a windmill in a tornado. He fended off the blows that backed him up against the porch railing. Reaching through the raining fists, he caught McGruder with both hands on the back of his neck and shoved down hard. At the same time he came up with a knee.

McGruder shuddered and lurched backward. Blood gushed from his nose and splattered the ground. The big man rolled over, stunned, then shook it off and stood again. Now there was nothing but a blind fury behind those hammering fists. McGruder backed Ketcham into Ollfinger's horse and whaled into him. The animal shied.

Ketcham threw up his arms to protect his face, leaving himself open below. McGruder's fists were rock hard and unrelenting. Ketcham sagged and tucked his elbows. He winced as blows glanced off his ribs. Finally his fist found an opening and shot a short jab that connected with the sore place on McGruder's face.

A groan escaped McGruder and his hands reached instinctively for his face.

Ketcham came from below with a short, powerful uppercut that folded McGruder in half. He stabbed out a foot to brace himself and drove in with a powerful left hook, spinning McGruder around. A rock-hard fist went into McGruder's kidney, and the big man teetered. Ketcham swung a leg, kicked out his pins, and McGruder went down hard and stayed there.

Ketcham hovered over him, his fists stinging, his ribs aching, his face burning and raw. But the fight was over. McGruder struggled to his hands and knees, then fell back, his fingers clawing the hard earth.

Jeb Ollfinger, still ramrod straight and clenching the saddle horn, leaned slightly forward and speared Ketcham with a narrow look. "That's enough." The scowl had left his face, making it flat and unreadable.

Ketcham nodded and backed off. "Get him out of here."

"Halstead, Wonderly, put him on his horse." Mild disappointment marked Ollfinger's voice. He considered Ketcham with thinly masked curiosity as his men picked up McGruder and helped him into the saddle. Bent and hurting, McGruder made an effort to haul himself straight. A final show of bravado. He had his pride, and Ketcham had dusted it twice. He'd not seen the last of Case McGruder.

Ollfinger shifted his view to Corely. "This doesn't change a thing, Mattlin." He looked back at Ketcham. "You're a fair hand with your fists, mister. And you got grit. I like that. A man like you I'd rather have fighting with me than against. When you decide to quit this outfit and take a job with real men, come by the ranch and we'll talk."

Ketcham managed a tight, painful grin. He glanced at the three faces of Ollfinger's men glaring at him. "That would be sorta like sticking my neck into a bear trap, now wouldn't it?"

Ollfinger considered Ketcham's glance, and his men. "If I give the word, you won't have no trouble from them."

"I'll keep that in mind."

The look Ollfinger gave Corely was harder than a Minnesota lake in January. "We aren't finished with this yet, Mattlin." Turning his horse, he rode away, his men following.

Ketcham looked back to discover Mrs. Mattlin glaring. Her worried look softened as he staggered a step toward the porch railing and grabbed onto it.

"You're hurt." She took in the cuts and bruises on his chest, where raw skin showed each rib. "Come into the house, Mr. Ketcham. I'll dress those cuts." Her manner had warmed decidedly, and he wasn't sure he'd made the best choice. He didn't want her thinking he'd changed his mind.

Corely followed. "Figured there'd be trouble." He shook his head.

Inside, she grabbed down a bowl from a cupboard and filled it with warm water from a pot on the stove. She had a lump of green soap in one hand and a clean towel in the other. He sat in a chair at her bidding and let her scrub the open cuts. The lye soap hurt almost worse than had his tangle with McGruder, though she tried to be gentle. He didn't complain. The fight had upset her more than she wanted to let on. He sensed her anxiety in her quick movements, her sharp breathing, her sudden silence as she cleaned the cuts and dabbed on a pungent salve.

What had happened between him and McGruder had nothing to do with the Mattlins. It was two men settling their differences. That was all. He wasn't Margaret Mattlin's savior, or anyone else's. He tried not to think about their troubles . . . about Mrs. Mattlin. But it was impossible to ignore the touch of her fingers upon his skin as she worked the salve into the abrasions.

Corely hovered near the window, looking out it from time to time.

"Got a clean shirt?" she asked when she'd finished tending the scrapes.

"No."

"I'll wash the one you were wearing."

"It's still out back." He stood, feeling aches in his muscles he hadn't noticed before. "I'll fetch it for you."

"I'll go with you," Corely said.

Ketcham put the rifle into the crook of his arm and walked stiffly back to the stand of cottonwoods.

Corely was unnaturally silent as they went. Whatever was on the old man's mind, he was having a hard time getting the words out.

"Does he treat all the farmers like he does you?"

Corely kept his view bent toward the ground ahead. "He don't cotton to any of 'em, but Ollfinger's got a particular hatred for me and Margaret."

"I got that impression." He levered the rifle over his shoulder. He was moving like an old man—like Corely—but the walking helped loosen his muscles.

A long frown pulled at Corely's face. He considered a moment, then nodded. "I'll show you."

He led the way to the seep Ketcham had noticed the day before; it was moist and spongy underfoot. "Water is a precious thing in this land, Ketcham. Something men would kill over."

It was an old fact of life. Ketcham understood it as well as any man who had raised cows or planted seed. Back in Arkansas and West Texas; water had never been a concern. But here, in this parched land, it was worth more than gold—it was worth the blood of men.

Corely stood a moment, then pointed at the field partly cleared for the plow. "See that? Looks greener than the rest of this dry land, don't it? That's what's called sub-irrigated. It means there's water just under the surface. Put down seed in that ground and crops would grow like weeds."

Ketcham studied the land, then glanced back to Corely's planted field where there was no water. "Good land . . . for farming. Why didn't you plant this first?"

Corely frowned. "I was foolish enough to think I could keep Ollfinger from breathing down my neck if I let the ground stand unbroken for a few years.

"Ollfinger? What's he got to do with it?"

"Come and take a look yonder."

Ketcham snatched his shirt off a low tree limb and followed Corely across the field toward an outcropping of shaley rock where the ground appeared to drop steeply away. Corely marched out to it and stood on the edge looking down, and all at once Ketcham understood why Ollfinger wanted Corely's land so bad. Was showing him this what had been on Corely's mind all along? The ledge dropped away twelve or fifteen feet, and from the cracks in the rocks a dozen small seeps trickled over the shelving into a natural tank maybe an acre or two across.

There are two things a cow needs to be happy: grass and water. This part of the Territory had plenty of the first, but it was mighty shy on water. What Corely had was a gold mine to a cattleman. Ketcham gave a soft, heartfelt whistle. "No wonder."

Corely shook his head. "I offered to let Ollfinger water his cows. A nickel a head for the season. Fair price, I reckoned. I warn't out to make a lot of money, but I figured I ought to be paid something. We ain't got much money, you understand."

"He didn't want to pay it?"

"It's not like he can't afford to. At one time he watered his cows here, only it warn't on his deeded property. The folks who owned this before us staked a claim and took out papers. Ollfinger run them off like he's trying to do to us. He could have bought this land legal and proper, but to do so would've been to admit he really didn't have squatter rights to it like he claimed. When we bought it, that made him all-fired mad. He figured he could run us off like he done them other folks. But he's wrong. I ain't a-leaving, Ketcham, and that's that. I tried to play fair, and what did he do? He sent his hired guns our way.

He killed my—" Corely stopped, then drew in a determined breath. "No sir, I ain't a-leaving."

Ketcham studied the clear pool. Corely had strung two strands of wire around it to enclose a small pasture of a few acres. "You do that wire?"

"Ollfinger was gonna put his cows in there anyway. So I stopped him. Figured maybe I might pasture a milk cow down there myself."

He frowned. "Seems to me you two could work out some kind of arrangement."

"Maybe at one time we could have. That's why I held off planting it at first." He swept his arm back toward the field he'd begun clearing. "But once I put that land to seed, the crop will suck the water out of that ground. This pool will likely dry up to a mud hole come the summer months. Ollfinger knows it, too. It's why he's pushing hard at me now, trying to keep me from finishing my work." Corely shook his head. "It's too late for making arrangements, Ketcham."

"He'll drive you out, or he'll kill you."

"Then I'll die. I've already buried two of the finest people the Lord ever put on this here green earth. I'll take my place at their side if need be. There ain't no other place I care to go now."

Those were strong sentiments, and he admired Corely for expressing them. How many times had he pulled out because troubles came and there wasn't enough in it for him to stay? Just the same, he figured Corely foolish for throwing away a good life to someone like Jeb Ollfinger. Corely was plainly a fighting man, but could he stand up to someone like Ollfinger and his boys? He grimaced. This was all going to come to a bad end. . . . He was suddenly thinking of Mrs. Mattlin. She'd die too, and maybe suffer worse than all the rest, if he understood men like McGruder and Wonderly like he thought he did.

Back at the house, Mrs. Mattlin had cooled her anger and steadied her nerves. She took his shirt and gave him another to wear. It was a mite tight across the shoulders and some short in the sleeves, but she nodded with approval and said it would do until his was washed. They ate a lunch of boiled potatoes, beans, and turnip greens. Then she made a fresh pot of coffee, and over a second cup Corely asked Ketcham how he was coming with his work.

"Expect I'll have that wood in by tomorrow or the next day."

"Then what, Mr. Ketcham?" Mrs. Mattlin made it sound casual, but her eyes were unblinking and her jaw had taken a hard set. When Ketcham looked at her, she glanced away.

"I'll move on."

"Ollfinger offered you a job," she said.

"I won't work for Ollfinger."

Corely's eyes compressed and studied him like he was a curious track in the ground that he'd come upon.

"I already told him," she said, somehow reading the question on Ketcham's mind.

Ketcham gave a small smile. "Sorry. Didn't figure you needed a cowpuncher on your property."

"I need a liar a lot less."

He stood and set his coffee cup on the table. "I'll be pulling out soon as I get the rest of that wood cut, Corely."

"On to your greener pastures?" There was a barb on the end of Mrs. Mattlin's words, though she'd spoken them gently.

"Probably." He didn't much care to have his decisions questioned.

"You don't have to go right away." Corely had developed a nervous tick at the corner of his mouth, and his gaze shifted away. "Maybe I'd have done the same thing if I was in your shoes. I'm a sinning man like everyone else, and have no right casting the first stone."

If Corely was a sinning man, Ketcham figured his own life made him a first-rate candidate for the world down below. If there was such a thing. He remembered as a child being dragged off every Sunday to church, where Preacher Dunsbury would rail on about the torments of Hell and how everyone was heading there unless they went and got themselves saved. It later turned out that Dunsbury and a married woman named Ethal Grooms were secretly seeing each other, and the scandal drove Dunsbury out of the county. There was never any joy in his parents' church that he could remember. When he finally left home for good, he put all churchgoing behind him. He wanted none of that kind of hypocrisy in his life.

"Staying will only bring down more trouble on you, and you don't need that." It would bring more trouble on himself too, but he wasn't worried about that. His trouble with McGruder had gone too far already. He could up and leave, as he had in the past whenever trouble became too hot, too near. But for some reason this time, he didn't want to leave. He realized he was looking at Mrs. Mattlin. Could she see what he was thinking?

If forced to make a choice, he'd stand beside the Mattlins against Jeb Ollfinger. He still didn't like farmers or what they were doing to the land, but he liked bullies even less. He'd gotten himself between that rock and a wall, and the sooner he was away from there, the better.

Corely chewed his lips and pushed them into a frown. "You do what you have to, Ketcham."

It was more than he could decide without some serious thinking on the matter. "What I have to do is finish up with that woodpile."

The sun was slanted to the west, still and hot when he left the house, but there was shade under the tall trees. Once again he set to sawing and splitting. Working helped keep his bruised muscles from tightening down on him. Maybe Mrs. Mattlin was right. Maybe there were no greener pastures. Maybe what folks longed for was only a notion concocted in their heads. Thinking back on his own travels, one place never really had been much better than the one he had left behind, and he'd left a lot of places behind since waving good-bye to his ma and pa.

It was growing up a farmer that had turned him sour on that kind of life, just as Dunsbury had soured him on religion. His thoughts drifted back to Mrs. Mattlin and the way she worked to keep her house, and took care of Corely. There was something solid in her . . . something reliable that a man could count on. He was confused.

He swung that ax blade deep into a round of wood and strolled over to the seep. The ground was cool to the touch, and he could feel the moisture when he pressed his palm to it. Water was a precious commodity out here. When a man had land where water came right out of the ground without having to pump or ditch for it, that was something of great value. Something to hold on to and fight to keep.

He glanced out across the field Corely had shown him. It was about the greenest thing he had ever seen this side of Amarillo. With a lot of work, it could be corralled and broken, and made to grow just about anything. A greener pasture?

Grimacing, he stood abruptly and strode over to the ax, wrenching it from the log and going back to work.

Chapter Seven

He caught sight of her out of the corner of his eye coming from the house. She stopped a few dozen feet back. "Mr. Ketcham?" she called tentatively, eyeing the rifle against the tree. "It's me."

She learned quickly. He grinned, buried the ax blade in a log, and straightened, his lungs heaving and his muscles burning. It felt good. "Come on in, Mrs. Mattlin."

She carried a wooden bucket, the handle of a ladle sticking out of it. "A man working hard as you needs more than a glass of water."

He grinned and fetched out a drink. Then he poured another ladle of water over his head. It ran cold over his face onto his chest and shoulders, and chilled his sweating skin.

She glanced at the pile of wood he'd already laid in and seemed impressed. "This will be such a help to Corely. He tries, but he just can't work as hard as he once did. He's got a bad back, you know."

"I've noticed him favoring it. Comes a time when even the strongest of men must face the truth. We don't go on forever."

"No. We don't—not in this world." Her face went flat. She looked out across the green, partly cleared field. "These last two years have been particularly hard on him—on us."

"Because of Ollfinger?"

She nodded. "You have a family, Mr. Ketcham?"

That took him by surprise. "I've a ma and pa, and two brothers. They're all back in Arkansas. Got no family of my own."

"Sometimes it's easier that way."

"What is?"

"Not having. Not ever having is easier than losing them after you've had them."

"You speaking of your husband?"

She kneaded her fist and stared at the sweet potato field across the way. Corely was out in that patch, working the furrows with a hoe. "We've only got each other now. It wasn't so when we came out from Kansas."

By the sadness in her voice he understood something about her he hadn't known before. She had followed her dreams, and in so doing lost more than she'd bargained for. Now she was hunkering down, as a hurt cat sometimes does—staying low, licking her wounds, trying not to get hurt again.

"You've got a good piece of land here. I can see why Corely is so set on holding on to it."

"Can you?" Mild accusation edged her voice as she looked back at him. "We've invested more than money in it, Mr. Ketcham. We've paid for it in blood. *That* makes it worth holding on to." A deep anger smoldered just below the calm surface—a festering sore Mrs. Mattlin struggled to keep hidden from view. She turned her face away, not wanting to talk any more about it, and he wasn't going to press her. Mrs. Mattlin was a good woman, a woman whose feelings ran deep. He felt sorry for her, and for Corely too. He wanted to reach out and draw her into his arms, to comfort her. But he didn't, unsure of the feelings stirring within himself. In the past he would have saddled his horse and ridden away. Distance usually cured any notions of commitment he had. But something about this place—this woman—was different. Riding away wasn't something he wanted to do. What did he want to do?

Margaret Mattlin went back to the house. He'd almost asked her to stay a while longer, but successfully fought down that urge too. Taking up the ax, he resumed splitting firewood with renewed vigor, working out his frustrations on the logs.

The Mattlins' troubles weren't any of his affair. Ollfinger, Wonderly . . . McGruder, they were bullies, but it wasn't his job to rid the world of the likes of them. He made up his mind to leave once his obligation was done here. He'd finish the job in the morning and come nightfall be miles away from here. Mrs. Mattlin's green pastures aside, there had to be something better than getting himself involved in a land feud.

With the decision finally made, he figured he ought to feel better. So why was his heart still heavy, and the hollow in his chest still so dark and deep?

He finished for the day, strolled over to the single row of barbed wire, and leaned against one of the rickety fence posts. Corely was on the far side of the field, chopping around the rows of green plants with a hoe, bending now and then to yank out a weed. He'd planted those sweet potatoes so straight, it looked as if someone had drawn lines on the ground with green paint. Ketcham stood there awhile, watching the gentle manner in which Corely cared for those plants, as if they had feelings all their own.

King romped over and sniffed his boots.

"That's cows you're smelling." He scratched

the dog behind the ears. "Better get used to it. You're liable to be smelling a lot more of it if Ollfinger gets his way."

Corely looked up, saw him standing there, and started working his way over. He moved kind of slow and stiff, and when he reached Ketcham he leaned on his hoe for support and stifled a groan. "Finished up for the day, Ketcham?" He glanced to the reddening horizon. The low sun pushed his shadow far out into the neatly hoed rows of sweet potatoes.

"I'll have the job done in the morning. This work getting to you?"

Corely pressed a hand to the small of his back and tried to straighten up. "I sometimes throw it out of kilter. Then it's cob to pay till it gets to feeling better. Only thing that helps is time . . . and a spoonful of laudanum." He winced. "And I think I could use some right about now."

He helped the old man into the house. Mrs. Mattlin took one look at them coming through the door and frowned. "You put your back out again."

He got Corely into a chair.

"How bad is it?" She shook the washwater from her hands and reached for a towel.

"I think I done a good job of it this time. Get me my medicine, will ya?"

Mrs. Mattlin fetched down a bottle from a cupboard, but when she turned it over it barely filled one teaspoon. She lingered for the last few drops to drip from the lip, then gave it to him.

Corely scrunched up his face and shook his head at the taste. "I'll get to feeling better shortly now."

"We'll have to get more." She took the spoon from him.

"I'll go into town in the morning," Corely said.

"Riding on that wagon into town will only add misery atop of misery." She glanced at the bottle. "Should have got some when we were in town yesterday."

"Don't fuss about it. I'll be all right. There's no way of knowing when it will happen, and we can't afford to be buying medicine 'less it's needed."

"Last time you were laid up for a week."

He grimaced. "Can't afford a week away from my field. Weeds will take over."

Ketcham said, "I'll go into town and fetch him his medicine."

She looked at him. "It's not your problem, Mr. Ketcham." She set the bottle and spoon on the counter. "I can take the wagon into town in the morning."

She was an independent woman, and he didn't feel like arguing with her at the moment. "I better put the tools away before it gets dark." He collected Corely's hoe, and the ax and saw he'd been using, and put them away in the toolshed. Then he went to the barn and stretched out on his bedroll.

The soft hay was just the remedy he needed for his aching muscles. The red was fading from the darkening sky, he saw beyond the window. He closed his eyes and let his thoughts drift. He found himself wondering dreamily what life might be like with a woman at his side. A smile lingered momentarily before it transformed itself into a frown. A woman would put a stop to his traveling ways. The frown wavered. But then, maybe it would be nice to have someone to share his life with. Sometimes he grew weary of always being on the move. Lying there, his thoughts cut adrift, he began to question his decision to leave. Indecision had never been one of his faults, and it irked him now to be so uncertain of his next move.

He did decide one thing. He would go for Corely's medicine in the morning. With Ollfinger's men making trouble, he'd not want Mrs. Mattlin alone on that stretch of road to Carson. He remembered how she'd shied away from Wonderly. That man had set his eye on her, and it was plain she knew it and didn't want anything to do with him.

He shifted his shoulders and tail end, nestling deeper into the soft hay. Mrs. Mattlin, Wonderly, Jeb Ollfinger, Corely—life had suddenly become complicated.

He was drifting off when his nose twitched. He sniffed the air, then sniffed again. Fresh baked biscuits. He dragged a tongue over his dry lips; his stomach rumbled. He'd not eaten since lunch, and only a little at that. From the house came the low groan of the door opening.

"Mr. Ketcham?" Mrs. Mattlin called.

He got to his feet and leaned halfway out the window. "Right here."

She turned to the sound of his voice. "Dinner is ready."

He didn't need any more of an invite than that.

Corely was at his place at the head of the table. Three plates were set, and she'd spread out a new tablecloth, its creases not yet ironed out. Corely motioned him to one of the chairs.

"How's your back?"

"Tighter than a fiddle string, Ketcham, but it don't hurt no more." He grinned, enjoying the effects of the laudanum.

"It will start to hurt again in a couple hours." Mrs. Mattlin set out a basket of biscuits, a bowl of mashed potatoes, and a platter of carrots and greens, mixed among the legs and breasts of a couple prairie chickens. It was a tasty meal like Ketcham remembered his mother cooking back home on the farm. Mrs. Mattlin sure could fix up a batch of victuals to please a man's stomach. He was admiring her cooking when he noticed the yellow ribbon tied into her hair. It had not been there earlier, he was certain. He would have noticed such a thing, because it was a handsome flourish. She caught his look and smiled, holding his gaze a long moment.

He scooted his eyes back to the food, his face warming. That hadn't happened to him since he was a fifteen-year-old boy and little Mary Allen gave him a peck on the cheek at Ben Seidel's wedding reception. What was Mrs. Mattlin trying to do? Win his help through her wiles? He remembered how little Mary, at fifteen herself, had filled out real pretty, and maybe that was one of the reasons he had lit out of Crawford County a couple months later. Margaret Mattlin wasn't Mary Allen, but he sure wasn't any more eager to sit still now.

Ketcham had assumed he'd come to understand how to handle women since then, even though in truth he'd had little experience with the fairer sex. It was just something a man took for granted as he grew in years and confidence. But he sure didn't know how to handle Mrs. Mattlin.

After dinner Corely stood, bent over and stiff, and said he was going to take a pipe of tobacco out on the front porch.

Mrs. Mattlin began clearing the table.

Ketcham strolled outside with Corely and watched him pack the bowl. The flare of the match played upon Corely's gaunt face. He inhaled to get his tobacco burning, then his eyes steadied on Ketcham.

"She's been a widow for over a year. Margaret is a good woman. Dependable and true. She made my boy a good wife. A man could do a lot worse. Don't look so surprised, Ketcham. I seen the way you two was looking at each other."

"You must have been mistaken."

"Hmmph. Not likely." Corely shuffled to a chair and gave a low groan as he eased himself into it. For a moment neither man spoke, then Corely said, "Will you be leaving tomorrow, Ketcham?"

He was grateful the old man had changed subjects. The air had cooled and held the pleasant scent of sage. He leaned his forearms onto the rail and looked out over the dark field of sweet potatoes. "Don't know. You want me to go?"

"Can't ask a man to work for no pay, but I could use a hand stringing a couple more lines of wire around that patch."

Ketcham looked at him, and Corely must have seen his disapproval.

"That's right, Ketcham. I forgot. You ain't a freight hauler. You work cows. And cowmen don't have nothing to do with stringing wire. Why not take Ollfinger up on his offer? I hear he pays his men top dollar."

"I won't work for a man who has to hire guns to get his own way."

"And you won't work with a man who plows the earth and plants the seed, either." He grunted. "Well then, the way I see it, leaving is the best thing you can do."

Was Corely right? He kept his view toward the blackness beyond the feeble reach of lamplight through the windows. The door stood open, and from inside the house came the clink of dishes being cleared and put into a tub. This place had a settled, homey feeling to it, something he'd missed for many years—something he hadn't realized he missed until now. A funny stirring began inside his chest. Corely was right. Leaving was the best thing to do. But he'd already been through the arguments, and he still didn't know his own mind. That uncertainty was brand new and unsettling to him. He was a man who never had trouble deciding, or following through once a decision had been made.

The chair creaked, and Corely strained to lift himself from it. "I better go pitch some hay to my horses."

"Bent up like you are, you'd be hard-pressed to pitch peanuts into a can, let alone fork hay into a stall. I'll do it for you. I'm about to turn in."

Corely considered the offer with some hesitation. It was plain he wasn't a shirker. But he was hurting, and he must have seen the sense of it. He gave a wry grin, and his bony head nodded a couple times. "It's hell getting old, Ketcham. Someday you'll know what I mean."

"Old age is a good thing to strive for—considering the alternative." He grinned.

"Appreciate the help." Corely tried to straighten up but couldn't. Folded and looking older than his years, he hobbled slowly back into the house.

Ketcham fished out his pouch and papers, rolled a smoke, and leaned against the porch post to study the night. There wasn't much to see of the weedy yard beyond the pale reach of light from the window. Overhead bats flitted and dove, catching insects on the wing. The breeze was cool and pleasant, and he might have stood there for five minutes or fifteen. He was tired and it was showing, but still he waited.

Around the far corner of the house a light flickered, then brightened and shone out a side window, reflecting dully off the pump standing in the shadows beyond.

His cigarette burned down and he flicked it away. He'd worked hard and fought hard, and now his thoughts drifted and were not very clear. He was about to head to the barn, when her footsteps tapped lightly on the porch, stopping just beyond the door.

"How's he doing?" he asked, not turning.

"He's gone to bed."

"The rest will do him good."

"His back will stiffen up tonight. By morning he'll have a time of it just getting to the kitchen table."

He turned. She stepped closer, and suddenly her presence was overpowering and he was helpless against it. He'd have rather faced a dozen Case McGruders than one female who made his knees go to jelly and his stomach tie itself into knots.

He wanted to know more about her, and about Corely's son—her husband—and those two graves they'd visited yesterday. Instead he said, "This happen often?"

"A couple times a year." She moved to his side and stared into the night. "He tries to not strain himself, but there's so much work to do, and now that he has no one but me to help him . . ." She let that thought trail off, as if inviting him to ask about what had happened.

He wasn't normally schoolboy-shy around women. So why did *this* woman turn his stomach to jelly? "How did your husband die?"

His bluntness didn't take her by surprise. She'd been expecting it, had sought to draw it out of him, he realized. "He was murdered. By that bunch Jeb Ollfinger bosses." The words came out in a rush, as if they were all penned up inside her just waiting to bust loose.

He grimaced. "Sorry. What happened to the man who did it?"

"Nothing." Mrs. Mattlin crossed her arms and glared into the night. "They claim no one knows who did it, but of course they *would* say that, wouldn't they? I'm sure they're covering for the murderer. Men come and go who work for Jeb Ollfinger. The one who killed Hank—he was one of those drifters. The sheriff talked to them, but they're a tight-lipped bunch. There was nothing to go on, and it's a big country to take care of, so naturally nothing ever was done, and the murderer, he still goes free."

"What makes you think it was Ollfinger's bunch? Lots of drifters pass through this Territory." *And I'm one of them,* he thought wryly.

"Word gets out, Mr. Ketcham."

She was being evasive now. He played a hunch. "How does Wonderly figure into it?"

Her startled look told him he'd hit a nerve. Her eyes narrowed suspiciously. "What about Kit Wonderly?"

"He's got an eye for you, Mrs. Mattlin. And you two have had words."

She glanced away and stared hard at the black landscape. "Words?" She gave a short laugh. "There is only one word to describe Kit Wonderly. He's a *liar.* More than a liar, he's a scoundrel and worse."

There it was again, anger like a seething cauldron bubbling away just below the surface. He'd noted it the first night he arrived. And again when she'd brought him water earlier that afternoon. But unlike then, he probed deeper this time, somehow knowing where it would end. "He made advances toward you, didn't he?"

"That man has no decency, no respect for the marriage vows."

"And when you refused him, he began spreading his lies. And your husband heard these lies?"

"He could hardly help it. Everyone heard

them. A few even believed them." Mrs. Mattlin drew in a breath and exhaled sharply. "Hank, he never believed a word of it, but he couldn't stand by and have his wife's reputation sullied."

"Why would Wonderly want to do such a thing?"

She wheeled to face him, fury burning hot in her eyes. "I believe it was to provoke Hank. To give them the excuse they needed to kill him."

"Them?"

"Kit Wonderly and"—her view flicked briefly away from him—"and his friend."

"Why?"

"To stop him and Corely from clearing and planting that field, of course." Her chin jutted toward the dark, well-watered land that lay beyond the stand of cottonwood trees. "They knew Corely couldn't do all the work himself. But behind it all was Ollfinger. They were just his pawns."

"So they forced your husband's hand?"

"They provoked him all right, but not in the way they expected. Hank, he never carried a gun. Didn't even own one. But that didn't mean he didn't know how to defend himself." A glint of admiration briefly swept away the anger, but it faded quickly. "He challenged them to settle it like men, with fists. They had to oblige him or be called down as cowards. Hank, he took them on one at a time with the whole town watching, and left them both sprawled out in the street by the time it was over. Two weeks later Hank was dead—Hank and Dorothy." Her voice caught. "Kit Wonderly, he had a solid alibi, while that other one had already cleared out of the Territory a few days earlier. No one knew where he'd gone to, or so they claimed. But I believe they were only covering for him."

What if Mrs. Mattlin was right? She'd be hard-pressed to prove it now.

"I've just unburdened my soul to you, Mr. Ketcham. Now it's your turn."

He gave her a surprised look.

"What really happened back in Bailey?"

"I already told you." Her question had caught him off guard.

"Tell me again. Who was it you angered in your card game?"

"Just some wranglers. Benny Gellerman was one, Harold Reed another, and a new kid at the ranch, James Haseltine."

And where was it you said they worked?"

"A cow camp about five miles east of town. The Muleshoe outfit."

"The Muleshoe," Mrs. Mattlin repeated the name, her words not more than a whisper. She stood there a long moment staring into the night, then suddenly drew in a sharp breath as if she'd stopped breathing the whole while. "It's getting late. Good night, Mr. Ketcham."

"Night, Mrs. Mattlin."

She went to the door, stopped, and looked

back. Her sudden hardness momentarily softened. "Call me Margaret." A smile flashed briefly, then disappeared.

"If you want."

"I think I would like it."

"Then good night . . . Margaret."

As she walked away he remembered something else. "Oh, Margaret." He liked the sound of her name rolling off his lips. She turned and looked back at him.

"In the morning I'll be going after Corely's medicine."

She simply nodded and continued into the house. A right sensible woman.

Chapter Eight

Ketcham saddled his horse early and stopped by the house on his way out to pick up money for Corely's laudanum.

"There's two dollars here," Margaret said, carefully depositing a handful of coins on his open palm, "and a small list of some things we need . . . since you are going into town anyway," she added almost apologetically, handing him a slip of paper.

"Be back in a few hours." His mare was well fed and rested, and anxious now to be on the move again. From out on the main road, the Mattlins' run-down farm stood gray and sad in the distance alone among the washed-out sage and the dusty green of all those sweet potatoes. Beyond the house and leaning barn, past the stand of cottonwood trees, the faint splash of brighter green stood out clearly, but he couldn't see the rock outcropping and the clear pool of water below it.

As he studied the place, he couldn't help think that the Mattlins' farm had potential, lots of it, considering all that springwater running so close to the surface. The promise was there to grow a lot more than sweet potatoes and peanuts. With that seep and natural pond, it had potential for raising stock. There'd be need to feed them, of course, yet with open range still plentiful, a small cow/calf operation would not be out of the question. . . .

He gave a wry grin. The Mattlins weren't interested in growing cows, they were farmers through and through. Dirt-caked fingernails was their way of life, and this farm was their hope. But grit and determination alone couldn't keep hope alive in this harsh land. The place needed more than Corely and Mrs. Mattlin could give. Maybe if Hank Mattlin had lived . . .

He frowned at the thought taking shape in his brain. Even if Jeb Ollfinger did not succeed in running them off the land, Ketcham couldn't see either one of them still living here five years from now. They should have stayed in Kansas.

The morning was heating up, a warm breeze blowing and the taste of alkali in the air. Here and there stood colorless hovels of human habitation—folks like the Mattlins trying to make a go of it.

Where a two-rut track veered off the main road, he drew rein and rolled a smoke, considering. The Bar JO lay that way some miles. No sign of Ollfinger's cows today. Ollfinger was a determined man too, but he had money and men behind him. It made a difference.

When the church came into sight, something compelled him to turn aside. Reverend Johnson's carriage wasn't there, and he felt it was safe to poke around the place some. Although the windows stood open a few inches and the front door was unlocked, not a soul appeared at the hollow echo of his boots on the plank floor. He halted before reaching the pulpit and looked around. There had been a time when church and Sunday mornings had been as natural as bread and butter . . . before he had left home. Even so, he'd never made the sort of commitment his mother and father had kept pushing for, and after Reverend Dunsbury had proved unfaithful, he completely turned away from anything that smacked of church and piety. Since leaving Arkansas, he'd hardly laid eyes on the inside of a church.

Out the side door and down the steps, he made for the boneyard. It was a small patch of dry ground, encircled by a low black iron fence that appeared almost too fancy for such plain surroundings; it was an expensive enclosure for not so many stone markers. His lips formed a wry smile. Civilization was still too young in this land for it to have produced a very large cemetery.

He spied the two graves where wilted bundles of flowers lay. The name *Hank Mattlin,* etched in a slab of yellow stone, marked one grave. *Dorothy Mattlin* had been chiseled into the stone of the second grave. The days of their birth were different, separated by twenty-two years, but the day of their deaths was the same. He frowned. Dorothy Mattlin. Mrs. Mattlin had mentioned the name. A mother? A sister? Corely's wife? And what had happened on April twenty-seventh, a little over a year ago?

The standing stones were silent on the matter.

A little while later, still pondering on the fate of the Mattlin family, he rode into Carson. The little town baked sleepily beneath the hot sky, and few folks moved along the timbered sidewalks that faced some of the buildings. The ring of a hammer beating a slow tempo against an anvil lingered in the air as he rode by the livery. The breeze carried the tangy odor of burning charcoal. A brood of chicks scrambling behind a clucking hen scampered across the street in front of him, while a pig snorted somewhere down one of the side streets. The thump of a chair briefly drew his eye toward a gent taking a siesta on the boardwalk. A few wagons and maybe a dozen horses were scattered up and down the street, and that was all. No one appeared interested in a stranger riding into their town. He turned toward the hitching rail in front of Hawkins's general store and tossed the reins a couple turns around it.

Horace Hawkins glanced up from behind a counter where a newspaper lay spread open upon the glass top. His white shirt had lost its tie, and the two buttons at his throat were unfastened. His eyes widened some as Ketcham came through the door, then a broad smile puckered his cheeks. "Don't hardly ever see folks from the hinterland into town twice in one week."

With the creak of wood and the thump of his cane, Hawkins lighted off a stool, came around the counter, and stood there, leaning on his walking stick. "Looking for another piece of pocket money?" He grinned, his bushy eyebrows lifting questioningly. "Sorry, but I'm plum out of odd jobs."

"Not looking for work today, pard. Running an errand for the Mattlins."

"Ah," Hawkins's eyes brightened, "then it's capital you intend to spend rather than earn!"

He tapped his vest pocket in a meaningful way and extracted the list Margaret had given him. Hawkins glanced it over, then looked up at him. "Corely's back giving him misery again?"

"He threw it out yesterday."

Hawkins shook his head. "Well, I've got everything here 'cept the laudanum. That you'll have to get from the druggist." He set about to gather up the few items.

"Where would I find one?" He didn't recall seeing a druggist's sign in town the last time he'd been here.

"Ned Wheely, the barber."

"Barber?"

"Not much call for medicines—not enough to support a druggist. Barbering brings in more money. Wheely, he went to school somewhere back east. He knows what he's doing."

Hawkins packaged up Mrs. Mattlin's purchases in brown paper and pushed the bundle across the counter.

Ketcham paid him, pocketed the change, and headed for the barber's shop, which was across the street and three buildings down from the One Stop Saloon.

"Mr. Ketcham," a familiar voice boomed.

He swung around. Reverend Liam Johnson, now wearing a leather apron, waved to him from the blacksmith's shanty against the livery. One big hand clutched a hammer, and the other held tongs in the glowing coals of an open furnace.

Ketcham walked over. "A smith?"

A smile stretched Johnson's coal-bin beard. "The church is too small to support a full-time minister. I've got to make a living for me and Susan somehow. Paul made tents. I shape iron and shoe horses."

"I'd never guess." Ketcham recalled the prissy

man who had pastored the church back in Arkansas. Dunsbury would have never dirtied his hands to earn an honest living.

"Just goes to show you can't judge a man by appearances." He stuck out a hand.

Ketcham took it, feeling the strength in it again. He could more easily picture Johnson a smith than a preacher.

"I didn't expect to see you again so soon."

He told Johnson about Corely's back. Johnson nodded, as if the old man's affliction was a commonly known fact.

The sound of a buggy rounding the corner drew their attention. Susan Johnson pulled back the reins and set the brake. She smiled when she recognized him. "Mr. Ketcham. Good to see you."

"Likewise, ma'am."

"Are Margaret and Corely in town?"

"No, ma'am. I'm just running a few errands for them."

"Corely threw his back out again." Johnson took the horse by its harness and steadied it as Mrs. Johnson stepped down from the carriage.

She brushed at the wrinkles in her blue cotton dress. "I'm sorry to hear it."

"I'll run out and drop in on him later today, or tomorrow." Johnson said.

Susan turned toward her husband with something else on her mind. "It's almost time. I've just come into town to get," she hesitated, cast a quick eye at Ketcham, then back at Liam, "a few things Betia might be needing."

"That's fine."

She looked back at Ketcham, a hint of color glowing in her cheeks. "It was nice seeing you again."

"Likewise, ma'am."

Susan Johnson retrieved her handbag from the floor of the buggy and left for Horace Hawkins's store. Johnson tied the horse to a rail, then moved back to the forge and pumped a bellows a couple of strokes, sending sparks flying from the open furnace. In spite of his bulk, Johnson carried little fat. The man was tall as a door frame, all muscle and ox-strong. Seeing him this way, Ketcham had a hard time picturing him as a preacher, but then he didn't know many churchgoing men—preacher or otherwise, and Dunsbury was a poor example to draw conclusions from.

"It's Betia MacRae," Johnson said. "Susan is going to midwife her."

"Ah." No wonder she'd been skittish. Margaret, now, would have come out with it—and probably expected him to help somehow.

Johnson grinned. "This will be Betia's first, so Susan's not sure what to expect. Chancy business, especially out here. But God made women strong that way."

He merely nodded. Not all women were strong that way. His aunt Beth had died birthing her

106

first. He thought of Margaret again. She had no chance at kids now with Hank taken so soon.

"You might tell Margaret."

He looked over with a start. Had the preacher read his thoughts?

"She'd want to know. You know how women can get where babies are concerned."

Ketcham laughed, but an unfamiliar feeling settled in. How would it be for a widow alone with an old man to see another woman's family begin, with all that meant . . . in a woman's mind, anyhow?

Johnson worked the bellows, turning the iron rod in the bright coals. "I figured you'd be on your way by this time."

"Took on some chores to pay my keep. I'll be pulling out once they are done." The words sounded right, but saying them brought a tightness to his chest. He wasn't as keen on leaving as he had been only a day before.

"Well, if you're still around come Sunday, I'd be pleased to see you at church." Johnson's words sounded sincere, and his smile appeared warm and honest as a summer's night, but he was setting the jaws of a trap, and Ketcham wanted nothing to do with it.

"I'm not much of a hand at going to church, Reverend."

"I'm not fire and brimstone, Mr. Ketcham, and I don't bite, either." Johnson grinned. "We got lots of fine folks in these parts, and most of them show up at church Sunday morning. Sometimes we even have cowmen and farmers sitting on the same side." He chuckled deep in his chest, his blue eyes glinting mischievously. "Surprising what it takes to get some folks together and civil. Come on and see for yourself. Got a few crusty old curmudgeons you just might take a liking to."

Ketcham laughed. "What kind of preaching would I get from a blacksmith? Might end up learning the finer points of fitting a shoe."

Johnson smiled disarmingly. He was an easy man to like, and that made Ketcham wary. "Well now, I sometimes get my best sermons from working the forge. Take this rod of iron, for example." He lifted it briefly from the coals and showed Ketcham the glowing end. "It's just about as hard and stiff as the backs of some sinners I know. You know the sort, Mr. Ketcham. Stubborn men who figure they can take on life on their own terms. But then life turns on them, like a rattlesnake. That's like the fire in my forge, you see."

He shifted the iron rod about in the sparking coals. "Yep, life gets mighty hot for them, and that's when they begin to see they really can't do it all on their own. That's when they are ready for the shaping hand of the Lord." He grabbed up the hammer, laid the piece of iron on the anvil, and struck it six or seven times. When he'd finished he'd formed a hook into one end of it.

"See, now this stiff-backed sinner is useful for

something." He admired his handiwork. "Yep, some of my best sermons come right from this forge." Johnson grinned, and the heavy hammer rang down upon the anvil. "I'll be looking to see you in church come Sunday, Mr. Ketcham."

Ketcham suspected he'd already been preached to and hadn't even seen it coming. He promised to consider it—if he was still in the area come Sunday. That seemed to satisfy Johnson. They said good-bye, and Ketcham bent his steps back toward that barber's shop.

The door to the barber's shop stood open to catch a breeze. Ned Wheely was taking a nap in the single barber's chair when the thump of Ketcham's boots startled him awake. He straightened up, adjusted the tilted pair of spectacles, and stared owlishly at Ketcham.

"Right here." He scrambled from the chair, patting the red velvet cushion.

"Didn't come for a haircut."

"A shave, then, of course. My, my, it has been a while."

Ketcham stroked the sandpaper at his chin and allowed that it had been quite some time since he'd felt the edge of a razor. "Afraid I haven't got the money for a shave. All I really come for is a bottle of laudanum. Hawkins says you sell the stuff."

"Horace sent you? You in pain?"

"It's for Corely Mattlin."

Wheely's owl-eyes expanded behind the thick lenses. "His back again?"

He was beginning to wonder if there was no one in Carson who didn't know of Corely's affliction. Wheely looked him up and down a moment as if trying to place him, then turned to a cabinet against the wall near the corner and opened it with a key. "New in town?" he asked, peering at the label of a bottle.

"Uh-huh."

"Friend of the Mattlins?"

"I'm helping some around their place."

He relocked the cabinet. "That will be forty-five cents."

Ketcham paid him, which left just enough of Mrs. Mattlin's money in his pocket for a shave . . . except the money wasn't his to spend. He hadn't thought to bring some of his own along. A shave would have felt good right about then.

"Thanks." He pocketed the bottle and started for the door.

"What about that shave?"

"Like I said, I'm flat broke today. Maybe next time."

Wheely gave a short laugh and swung his arm with a flourish. "As you can see, I'm just bubbling over with business."

Ketcham grinned. "I can see you're about as busy as a beaver in a dry hole."

"Climb into that chair, and don't worry about money."

"Why?"

"Why?" He blinked, and his lips screwed together thoughtfully. "Well, when my Ruby come down with the rheumatic fever, it was Maggie Mattlin who brought her food and stayed at her bedside cooling her brow and caring for her. And when Tally Gottlieb's house burned down, Corely and Hank were right there to help him rebuild it. The Mattlins have always been first in line when someone needed a helping hand. Now, when hard times come upon them, not many folks seem inclined to pay back. I feel different. There ain't much I can do, but Corely, he ain't paid for a shave or a haircut in my chair for a year now. It's a small thing and don't cost me nothing, but it helps when you got shallow pockets, if you know what I mean."

He knew. He slid into the oak chair and let Wheely wrap his face with a hot towel. It had been so long since he'd had a real shave, he'd almost forgotten the sheer pleasure of a warm towel and spicy lather.

Ketcham relaxed into the chair. "Who was Dorothy Mattlin?"

"Dorothy? She was Corely's wife. He didn't tell you?"

"I saw the name on her gravestone."

Wheely shook his head as the cool razor slid smoothly over the crags and crevices of Ketcham's chin. "Mother and son side by side in the cold ground. It shouldn't be so. Their deaths, they were a hard blow. They knocked the wind out of both Corely and Maggie."

Maggie. He couldn't quite pin that name on the woman he'd met. Too playful, too . . . but maybe she'd been that way before troubles had made her sharp. Maggie. Had Hank called her Maggie?

"How did it happen?"

"Careful lest you lose a hunk of skin." The razor stopped, then resumed its long, slow climb up his neck. "They was bushwhacked. All four of them. Corely, he took a slug in the bacon. It put him down for a week. Maggie, she was spared altogether. A miracle, considering. But Dorothy and Hank, they weren't so lucky."

He'd already heard part of the story from Margaret. She'd said the murderer hadn't been caught, but he wanted to hear what Wheely had to say about it. "Who did it?"

"Never did learn who done it. Some say it was Ollfinger's bunch, even though there never was any proof. The only real suspect had already pulled out of the Territory by some accounts."

"Some accounts? Whose accounts?"

Wheely's hand jerked back, and he snorted impatiently. "Nearly caught your dadburn Adam's apple that time, mister. Mostly it was by the word of a few of the Bar JO ranch hands. Kit Wonderly, he swore the fellow had pulled out for Texas a few days before."

"What about McGruder?"

"He backed up what Wonderly said, and so did the others. Even old man Ollfinger said it was true." Wheely gave a short laugh. "But I suspect Ollfinger doesn't know the half of what's going on. He puts too much trust in his men and his son. That boy of his, he's heading down the wrong trail if you ask me, and his pa, he don't even see it."

"Isn't Ollfinger bent on running the farmers off the range?"

"He'd like to see them go, it's true, but I don't think he ordered all the heavy-handed means his boys use."

"You mean murder?"

The razor momentarily stopped, then resumed its even glide up Ketcham's throat. "Ollfinger's not that sort of man. He's hard, and he's determined, but he's no murderer. Trouble is, he's hired on men who are. I've got the feeling there'll be more bloodshed before the matter works itself out. Got a feeling it ain't gonna get better until the government sends in a federal marshal to see to it."

Ketcham frowned. And long before any federal marshal had been summoned, the Mattlins would be driven off their land and Ollfinger would have won his battle.

He saw Margaret's face again telling him he'd been sent there for a reason. He understood her desperation; it took a mighty desperate woman to pin her hopes on Chance Ketcham. Not that

113

he couldn't handle what trouble came his way; he just made it a point to keep out of other folk's business. Corely and Margaret had taken on their fight breaking up that first chunk of sod. If it wasn't Ollfinger, it'd be someone else. Either way it didn't concern him, no matter what Maggie Mattlin might think.

Chapter Nine

By the time he left the barbershop, Reverend Johnson's missionary anvil was quiet and the big man was nowhere to be seen. Ketcham shifted Mrs. Mattlin's package under his arm and eyed his horse across the street. The morning had been pleasant and uneventful, and what Wheely had just told him was busying his brain. He didn't take notice of the man lingering at the corner of Wheely's building until it was too late—

He leaped for Ketcham and grabbed an arm. Ketcham dropped the package, instinctively twisting to his left. At the same time, a second fellow sprang from the alley and latched onto his right arm. He yanked the gun from Ketcham's holster and tossed it out into the street. Ketcham wrenched around, launching him through the handrail and into the street. He wheeled back, for the first time getting a good look at his first attacker.

Wonderly!

Somehow he wasn't surprised. His right arm now free, he drove hard into Wonderly's gut. Breath exploded from the man's lungs and he folded. Ketcham drew back for a short uppercut, but a pair of strong arms caught him from behind and dragged him back.

The fellow in the street scrambled to his feet and came charging back. Wonderly drew himself up, his breath coming in hard, short gasps, hate twisting his face as he lurched for Ketcham with clenched fists.

"Not here, Kit." It was McGruder's voice. Wonderly held back, the fury in his eyes shifting between Ketcham and McGruder.

The three of them dragged Ketcham kicking and fighting like a bearcat around the corner and down the alley. Something hard rattled Ketcham's brain and drove his teeth together. He sagged in their grasp as they dragged him around behind Wheely's barbershop. They hauled him over to a post and stood him against it, two of them pulling his arms back and around the post until his shoulders cried out.

Standing to one side was Thad Ollfinger, grinning, but glancing around, worried-like.

McGruder strode into view. His mouth

twisted into a snarl as he stood there glaring. Purple and black splotches marred the left side of his face where Ketcham had hit him with the rifle, and his nose bulged angry red where his fist had broken it.

"I don't know how it is where you come from, but in these parts, butting in where you don't belong ain't a smart thing to do, mister.

He'd just been thinking that himself.

Wonderly said, "And sticking around after you done so wasn't very smart either."

McGruder's big knuckles ground into the palm of his left hand.

Ketcham's head had begun to clear, his vision sharpening a little. From where he stood, prospects for getting away in one piece were looking mighty dim. He tugged at the hands holding him, and fire burned along his shoulders. "I figured you for a man who didn't need help to fight his battles."

McGruder's reply came swift and hard, buckling him over. His partners yanked him straight again, slamming his head back against the post. Lights exploded behind his eyes, and for a moment he couldn't breathe. Slowly, painfully, his lungs began to fill with air. McGruder swung again, his knuckles digging at Ketcham's chin. Only rolling with the punch kept his jaw from shattering. Dazed as he was, he'd likely not be so lucky the next time.

McGruder reached down for something that

looked to be the broken handle of an ax. "Now I'm gonna hurt you real bad, Ketcham." He ran a thumb along the bruise on his eye and cheek, a thin smile cracking his hard face. He reared back with the stick.

Just then the back door to the barbershop slammed open and Wheely burst out, clutching a broomstick.

McGruder glared at the owl-eyed man. "Stay out of this."

"I saw it all. Let that man go."

"Honniger." McGruder snapped his head toward Wheely. "Take care of him."

"Hold him, Kit." One set of hands let go of his arm, while another set tightened its grip.

Wheely swung. The broom handle cracked. Honniger howled.

Wonderly released Ketcham, who slumped to the ground. He struggled to his feet.

McGruder wheeled around for him, the hickory club rising in his fist. "Oh no you don't."

Ketcham fell back against the post and tried to raise his arms over his head, but he might as well have been attempting to lift a hogshead of lard. McGruder swung, but the club stopped, frozen there in the air as if it had come against a brick wall. Then the club leaped from McGruder's grasp, a bear-size hand holding it. Liam Johnson loomed over McGruder, the wrath of God etched in the preacher's face.

"Playing a little rough, aren't you, Case?"

Johnson's voice had plunged lower than usual. His "sermon" voice, Ketcham mused in a vaguely detached way: a barrel-deep rumble that all by itself would slam the fear of God into a man.

McGruder backed up a couple steps. "Don't get involved in this, Johnson."

The preacher patted the hickory shaft against his open palm as if it were a mere feather in his hand. "I already am, Case." He glanced at Thad. "Your pa know what you're up to?"

Thad Ollfinger's eyes shifted from side to side and he started to speak, then hesitated. Pushing a cocky face at Johnson, he said, "Course my pa knows what I'm doing. And even if he didn't, I'm old enough to make my own decisions."

Johnson frowned. "You better look twice at the road you're heading down, son." He eyed McGruder again. "You and your friends take off now." The club stabbed out, stopping six inches from McGruder's swollen nose. "I mean now!"

Honniger and Wonderly looked to McGruder. Ketcham noticed that they were smart enough not to use their guns in town.

McGruder shot a burning glare at Ketcham. "We ain't finished with this yet."

Ketcham got his feet under him and stood, holding back a grimace as he rotated an arm. Maybe they weren't, but he'd be ready for them next time.

McGruder eyed his partners and jerked his head. The four of them strode back to their horses tied behind the saloon. They mounted up and rode off.

With a sudden lurch, Johnson flung the club far out into the tall grass field behind Wheely's place, then looked Ketcham up and down. "They hurt you bad?"

"Been hurt worse."

Johnson shifted his concerned eyes toward Wheely. "You okay, Ned?"

Wheely brushed the dust from his apron. "You come by just in time, Liam." He polished his spectacles on the sleeve of his white shirt and settled them in place. "I busted my new broom over Honniger's noggin, I did."

Johnson grinned. "You'll lose customers treating them that way, Ned."

"Aug Honniger? Hmmph! He never spent a nickel in my place."

Ketcham took a step and staggered. Johnson came alongside, helped him through Wheely's back door, and eased him into the barber chair. Strength slowly returned to his arms, and the deep ache in his gut began to lessen.

"You're lucky they didn't bust *your* noggin wide open, you are," Wheely said.

From the feel of it, he thought they already had.

"Luck had nothing to do with it, Ned." Johnson smiled knowingly, as if he'd been privy to some supernatural insight.

Maybe God and Johnson had just had themselves a powwow over what had happened. Ketcham frowned. Johnson. Margaret. They both seemed to have the inside track. The preacher preached even when he wasn't in the pulpit. He wasn't certain he liked Johnson very much just then. "I better get back." Standing out of the chair reminded him again of all the places he hurt.

Wheely brushed dust from his shirt and trousers. "You okay to ride?"

"I'm okay."

Wheely handed him the package and the revolver he'd rescued from the street in front of his shop. The laudanum still inside his vest pocket had somehow escaped damage.

Johnson held the door open for him. "I think I'll ride out to Corely's place too, just to see how he's faring with that back of his. Mind if I tag along?"

"It's an open road. You can go where you please."

Johnson strode back to the stable for his horse. Somehow, Ketcham wasn't surprised when the preacher led a big, gray Percheron from the wide door.

He didn't feel much like talking on the ride back. He was angry at McGruder, and at Johnson for his preaching ways, but mostly at himself for being caught flatfooted. It wouldn't happen again! And he'd be damned if he'd hide behind some preacher's tails. Even if the man did stand nearly seven feet tall and had arms like a bear, and Ketcham's own head was still fuzzy.

Thinking it over, there was no good reason to be chafing at Johnson, except for his constant, offhanded references to the Almighty. He was in no mood to be preached at, yet Johnson seemed determined to serve him up a steady diet of it. The ride helped blunt his anger. McGruder and his boys kept shy of them the whole way, which was smart on their part considering Ketcham's short-fused mood. His gun hand never strayed very far from his revolver.

From a chair on the porch, Corely watched them ride up the lane. He stood stiffly, bent over, and leaned both hands on the railing. "Afternoon, gentlemen." His gaze lingered on Ketcham's face. "You look like a man who's not had a good day."

"I've had better." He gingerly touched the fresh knuckle-rash on his chin. "How's the back?"

"It hurts."

"Ketcham told me you threw it out again," Johnson said.

Ketcham leaned over in the saddle and handed him the laudanum. "This will help."

"Hurt it good pulling up them weeds." Corely looked back at Ketcham. "What did you do to your chin?"

"Walked into a fistful of knuckles."

Corely frowned. "Bar JO boys?"

He nodded.

"Who was it?" Mrs. Mattlin asked.

He turned to find her standing in the doorway. "You creep up on a man quiet as an Injun, ma'am."

Johnson said, "It was McGruder and Wonderly, and that other fellow who hangs with them. Honniger."

"Are you all right?" Sudden concern came to her face.

"A little worse for wear, but I'm okay. They caught me wool-gathering. It won't happen again."

Her fists clenched and a scowl darkened her face. "Something ought to be done about Mr. Ollfinger's bullies."

"Yes, ma'am."

All at once her expression changed; her eyes widened and a smile touched her face. "You have gotten a shave, Mr. Ketcham."

His hand went to his cheek. "Wheely insisted."

"Good for Ned."

He didn't like the light he saw in her eyes. He wasn't a vain man by nature, but he knew he cleaned up well enough. He didn't need more reasons in her mind that he should stay. But doggone if her smile didn't stoke his insides.

Johnson said, "Susan wanted you to know that Betia is getting ready to deliver soon. She's buying what's needed."

123

Margaret's face brightened. "Did Susan say how soon?"

Johnson's big shoulders rolled beneath his coarse shirt. "How does a body know about something like that for sure? But I got the feeling tomorrow or the next day there's going to be a new member of the church." He grinned.

"I must bake something to bring it to Betia and Ed."

Ketcham dismounted and opened the saddlebag. "Here is your package, and the money left over."

She took them from him, beaming at the news of Betia's soon-to-be-born baby, and went back inside the house. Corely merely shook his head and grinned.

Ketcham spent the rest of the afternoon with Johnson and Corely. He hurt all over and just wanted to rest out the day. Johnson left a few hours later, and afterward, Corely and he whiled away the remaining daylight on the porch, smoking, talking, watching the summer shadows lengthen across Corely's sweet potatoes.

He ate dinner with the Mattlins and crawled off early to his bedroll. The next morning he walked the perimeter of Corely's land, tossing a stick for King, who romped ahead of him. He studied the pool below the seep, went back for a bar of soap, and spent a half hour in the water scrubbing himself clean. He soaked his clothes and washed them, too. With no towel, he lounged against the rock ledge, letting the sun warm his bruised body. He napped, then dressed in his still-damp clothes. He wandered back to the barn, brushed his horse, watched a hawk circle above the trees, cleaned and oiled his gun. Even the most mundane distraction seemed appealing—anything to keep him from the woodpile.

Come noon, he knew he was dragging his feet. There wasn't that much work left to do, so why didn't he just finish it up? He spent more time than necessary, putting a fresh edge to the ax, then, slinging the saw over his shoulder, he made his way back out to the stand of trees and went to work.

He was chopping the last of the promised two cords of wood when he heard it. The low, dull rumble was a far-off sound at first, and might have been dismissed as distant thunder by someone who didn't know any better. But the sky was clear, and he knew better. He'd heard that *thunder* before—on peaceful nights when a sudden noise or an unfamiliar odor sparked fear in the minds of cattle. He'd heard it in the middle of the day, too, on hot, dusty drives.

The rumble grew louder, and now a faint tremor began working up through the soles of his boots. He flung the ax aside and, grabbing up his shirt, raced for the corral. In a moment he had his horse saddled, yanking the cinches tight as the first ominous clouds of dust smudged the skyline beyond a ridge of land no more than a hundred rods behind Corely's sweet potato patch.

Corely and Mrs. Mattlin rushed out onto the porch, peering at the rising dust cloud. Corely cocked his head, listening to the rumble growing louder by the second. Ketcham kicked the corral gate open and leaped into the saddle. His horse jumped into a gallop.

"Get back inside the house!" he yelled as the horse streaked past the two of them. Not looking back to see if they'd heard him, he dug in his heels and reined off the lane, pounding out across the tall grass toward the dust cloud roiling off the ridge.

A dozen men couldn't stop a stampede. What did he hope to accomplish? Turn them? Maybe get himself trampled to death? With the horse lunging beneath him, he settled his thoughts. Stopping them was out of the question. Turning them, maybe just a little, was what he must do. He found himself whispering a few words for help, and immediately dismissed the notion. A fleeting image of a burning red forge swept through his mind and was gone. Reverend Johnson was getting under his skin.

He shoved thoughts of the preacher aside and, with iron resolve, set his mind to try the impossible. The dust cloud swelled as he drew closer, the thundering roar building just beyond the ridge. All at once a wall of rampaging cows burst over the crest, hooves pounding, great, pointed horns glinting in the sunlight. They rushed down toward the Mattlins' homestead. He yanked the reins and cut sharp to the right, straight across the path of the raging animals, and streaked for the stampede's left flank. Running flat out, the horse seemed to anticipate his intentions. She turned on a pivot at his touch, and the next instant they were running alongside the herd, drawing close to the lead animals.

He fired his revolver into the air.

The crazed animals barreled straight on, hardly flinching at the crack of the gun. Taking a chance, he moved in close to the lead animals. If the horse stumbled now, they'd both go down under those slashing hooves. But the mare was surefooted and big-lunged, and she held her place with uncanny cow sense, shifting left and right with the stampede as if reading their minds. He kicked out, driving his heel into the shoulder of the lead cow, but he might as well have been trying to turn a locomotive.

Urging the horse on, he moved a little ahead, cutting across the cows' path once more. Now in front of them, he fired again. That caught their attention, and they seemed willing to take his lead, for the first time shifting their trail of destruction a little to the right. But it was coming too late. Corely's cultivated acreage was looming larger ahead, and just beyond it were the house and outbuildings—

The sudden report of a rifle shot cracked above the crashing hooves. The zing of a bullet rang past his ear. He ducked and cast about over his shoulder, spying a man on horseback up on the ridge. In glimpses, he watched him put a rifle back to his shoulder and draw a bead.

He yanked his horse around and buried his heels. The rifle cracked again. He charged back around the side of the stampede and up the ridge. The man held his place a few moments, as if stunned to see Ketcham coming toward him. Realizing his mistake, he reined around and put spurs to his horse.

Ketcham leaned low, kicking his heels. He'd failed to turn those cows, and there wasn't anything more he could do. But the one responsible wasn't going to get away. The two horses flew up over the ridge and down the other side. The ambusher, still holding his rifle, bent to the rushing wind and dug with his spur demanding more speed from his animal. But the horse was no match for Ketcham's big mare. In half a dozen minutes the distance between them had shrunk. The man glanced back.

Honniger!

Bile climbed into his throat. He gritted his teeth, grinding back his anger, determined to run Honniger down even if doing so took him all the way back to the Bar JO.

Losing ground, Honniger twisted in his saddle, swung his rifle, and fired. He worked the lever and fired again. Offhanded like that, his bullets went wide. His fourth shot put lead close enough for Ketcham to hear it crack the air. He opened the distance between them a mite. Any closer and Honniger might get lucky.

As if suddenly realizing he was going to lose this contest, Honniger reined his horse around and charged straight for Ketcham, pushing his rifle into his shoulder and taking aim. The report and white puff of smoke came together. Ketcham's horse flinched aside.

Ketcham drew his revolver. The two men were almost upon each other now. He leaned off the side of his horse as Honniger flew past. A bullet whined over his head.

Ketcham twisted back and fired. Honniger lurched to one side and dropped the gun, then folded forward and clutched for the saddle horn. Reins dragging the ground, the horse slowed, then trotted to a stop.

Ketcham circled wide, drawing in cautiously, his revolver ready. Slumped over in his saddle, Honniger didn't move. Ketcham halted a dozen paces off. Honniger's head turned, his face drained of blood, watching through half-closed eyelids. Red streaks ran down the saddle and over the horse's withers.

"Where did you take it, Honniger?"

He just leaned there staring at Ketcham, bad

hurt and bleeding hard. Swinging down off his horse, Ketcham reached Honniger's side as the man's grip let go. Honniger slipped into his arms, and he lowered him among the sagebrush.

"Who set you up to this?"

Honniger stared up at him, blinking, a trickle of blood marking his chin.

"You're dying. No need taking extra burdens with you to the grave. Was McGruder in on this? Wonderly?"

He managed a nod. He was slipping fast.

"Did Ollfinger order it?"

He worked his lips, and his mouth formed a single, muted word, blood gurgling on his breath. "No."

That was a surprise, but before he had time to think it through, another question sprang to mind—one more urgent. "Mrs. Mattlin's husband. Do you know who murdered him?"

Honniger's eyelids were fluttering, but they opened wide at that.

"You do know!" Ketcham lifted Honniger's head to keep him from choking on his own blood. "His name! What's his name?"

The dying man's lips came together, trying to form a word. Only a single breathy syllable emerged. "Ga . . . Gell . . ." Honniger's eyes rolled up in his head and he went slack in Ketcham's arms.

He lowered the lifeless head back onto the ground. He'd been so close. The name had been but a breath away.... Ketcham heard their horses coming up fast behind him. A gun boomed and a bullet kicked up a spray of dust a few inches from his arm. He swung around, drawing his revolver and firing.

Wonderly grabbed at his arm and broke off his attack.

McGruder's revolver barked.

Ketcham fixed him in his sights.

McGruder's next shot went long.

They were less than fifty feet apart when Ketcham snapped off two rounds, putting them near enough to force McGruder to break off the charge and turn tail.

McGruder and Wonderly lifted a plume of dust in their retreat. A third man joined them at the crest of the rise. Thad Ollfinger.

Standing, Ketcham shivered as the rush of the battle ebbed from his body. Then he noticed the red smear down his horse's neck and went to her. Honniger's bullet had creased the mare. It wasn't serious. It could have been worse, much worse.... It could have been him.

He stared at the body at his feet and grimaced. He hadn't wanted to kill Honniger, but the man had left him little choice. He hoisted the dead man over the saddle and tied him there, then peered off in the direction McGruder and Wonderly had fled.

The Bar JO had raised the stakes, and Honniger was the first to cash in. Who would be next?

Chapter Ten

Corely's acres of sweet potatoes were gone, the wire snapped in a dozen places, the plants trampled beyond recognition. Ketcham rode down from the ridge and stopped to survey the damage. The house was still standing, but the corral had been swept away. The barn sagged dangerously, a corner of its roof tilting steeply to the ground. Three or four cows remained bunched up in a corner of the field where a post had held.

Margaret stood motionless upon the porch, the warm breeze moving with the hem of her skirt and teasing her long brown hair where it hung in tangles about her shoulders. She was too stunned to move. Corely wasn't anywhere to be seen. Ketcham urged his horse ahead with a tight lump growing in his gut.

Her head turned as he drew up, her eyes showing no emotion other than to widen slightly at the sight of Honniger tied wrist to ankle across his saddle.

"Corely?" Ketcham cast a worried look around the shattered farm.

She dragged her view off the body and nodded toward the sweet potato patch. Slumped to his knees, Corely was bent over something in that field of dark earth. Ketcham tied the horses and walked out to him. King romped to his side a few paces, then bounded curiously toward the cows.

Barbed wire sagged to the ground in a dozen places, and everywhere he looked was the green of shredded leaves, all mixed in with the dirt. Somehow a single plant had survived the massacre. Maybe others remained, too. How could one tell amid so much destruction? But Corely had found this one, and he was carefully tending it, scraping away the crushed leaves and stems and mounding the dirt back around the stem. If he heard Ketcham coming, he didn't show it, didn't waver from the task.

He hunkered down beside the old man. "Those cows sure played cob with your plantings."

Corely looked up, moisture rimming his eyes. "Gonna have to replant it all."

Even Ketcham knew it was too late in the season for that. "I'll help you." The words surprised him. When he'd left home all those years ago, he'd swore he'd never do farmer's work again. What could he be thinking now?

Corely stared at the single plant, then scrubbed his nose with a dirty fist. Ketcham glanced to the three cows caught in the corner of the field. "Not much more you can do today. Go back to the house and take care of that bad back of yours. I'll get rid of those cows."

He helped Corely to his feet. The farmer was bent over like an old, rusty nail. Ketcham stayed at his side as he hobbled to the edge of the field and paused a moment to stare at the sagging string of barbed wire. Shaking his bony head, Corely crossed to the house.

Margaret inclined her head at the man across the saddle. The question in her eyes was plain when she looked back at Ketcham.

"He didn't give me much choice. Tried to bushwhack me from the ridge."

"Too bad it's the wrong man" was all she said.

He knew what she meant by that, and it made her hard saying it. With very little urging, that woman could grow bitter.

Corely gave her a sharp look. She ignored it and helped him inside the house.

Ketcham moved Honniger back behind what was left of the barn, out of sight of the house, then rounded up the cows in the field and drove them out along the lane. Barbed wire and sharp horns had played devil with their hides. He ought to doctor them but had nothing to do the job. In the distance a couple stragglers had run themselves out and were peacefully grazing the tall grass. His herd grew to six, then ten, and by the time he'd closed a wide circle, eighteen of Jeb Ollfinger's cows were moving contentedly along ahead of him. It felt good to be working cattle again. Pushing them along, easy like this, he almost forgot what had brought it on. Frowning, he knew what he had to do next.

He moseyed them on down to the natural tank Corely had fenced off. Four more cows had stopped there, nosing at the wire, eyeing the sweet water beyond. He obliged them, pulling aside a wire gate and letting them all inside, where they had grass and water aplenty. They'd be in no hurry to go anywhere.

Margaret came out onto the porch as he rode up the lane. He drew to a stop and leaned forward. "How are you doing, Margaret?" She'd asked him to use her name, but it felt clumsy on his tongue. How would "Maggie" feel?

Sudden fury sparked in her eyes, and he wished he hadn't thought it. But her anger wasn't toward him. The shock of the stampede had worn off, and now she was more alive than he could remember. "I'm angry, Mr. Ketcham. I'm spitting mad angry! *That's* how I'm doing."

He grimaced at the venom in her voice. "And Corely?"

Douglas Hirt

Her tone softened. "Hasn't said much. He just sits at the window staring at that." Her finger shot out toward the ruined ground. "What will happen to us now? How are we going to make it through another year? He keeps saying he will start over. But he knows it's too late to put in another planting!"

"He'll come around." Those crops had once been their hope. Now they were gone. "The man who caused this needs to take the responsibility."

"Mr. Ollfinger?"

He nodded.

"That will never happen!"

He turned his horse toward what remained of the barn. Maybe she was right. Maybe Ollfinger was unreachable.

Grimly, he eyed the tottering barn, slipped out of the saddle, and ducked beneath the twisted door frame where dusty shafts of sunlight filtered down through rifts in the roof. His bedroll and gear lay beneath a cracked beam, undamaged. He rescued them along with the rifle he'd taken from Wonderly. Squeezing through a gap in the back wall, he emerged behind the barn where he'd left Honniger and took up the reins to the horse.

He cleaned the bullet crease on the horse's neck, putting salve on it, then wearily climbed back onto his saddle and started away. At the trampled field he drew up. His brow furrowed. He slipped from his saddle and strode along the

136

fence, examining the ends of the downed wire between the few standing fence posts. The breaks had sharp, clean edges and caught the sunlight like flecks of a mirror.

He frowned and returned to his horse, swinging back into his saddle.

Margaret came out onto the front porch. "Where are you going?"

"Pay Ollfinger a visit."

"No!" Sudden concern filled her face.

"The man owes you and Corely. I'm going to see that he pays up."

"He'll kill you." She rushed to the edge of the porch, her fingernails digging into the railing. "Just like he did Hank and Dorothy. You can't . . ."

"Someone has to put a stop to this."

"And you think you can?"

Wasn't she the one who first suggested it? Wasn't this what she had intended for him all along? "I can try."

She seemed to want to say more, but held back. He gave her a tight grin. "I'll be all right."

"You won't come back . . . Chance." That was the first time she'd called him by name, and by her hesitation he knew it had been difficult for her too. Their relationship had changed. The hopelessness in her voice rent apart the tight veil she had been keeping on her heart. Her concern ran deeper than merely his safety. Maybe Margaret really did believe he'd not be coming back.

Maybe Ollfinger would kill him, or maybe he might just keep on riding. That had always been the way he'd handled problems before, and she knew it.

"I'll be back."

She didn't reply at once. "Good-bye."

He turned away from the house and tried to put Margaret Mattlin from his thoughts, but he'd as soon try to put a whirlwind out of mind.

Jeb Ollfinger's headquarters rambled across four or five acres of flat land, made up of a scattering of buildings and the crooked lines of corrals. Each building appeared to have been shaped up with no regard to any of the others. He studied the place from afar before riding in . . . into a hornet's nest? A wry grin creased his face.

A small frame house painted white stood off to the left, its bright tin roof reflecting the late, hot sunlight. Another, smaller cottage sat a few rods behind the main house, shaded some by two large trees. Two barns stood back from the other structures, surrounded by a maze of corrals that snaked out toward the house. A medium-size log building among them might have been the bunkhouse. All these had been haphazardly tossed about the landscape. Nothing lined up; symmetry was disdained here on the Bar JO. It was hard to tell where the corrals ended and the yard proper began. Not a lick of grass grew near the house, or anywhere else among the buildings. Maybe the horses were allowed to graze the property unhindered?

A man stepped out of a small shack, crossed behind one of the barns, folded himself through a corral railing, and strode up to the house. McGruder. There was no mistaking that arrogant swagger. He knocked at the door and was let inside.

Ketcham clucked his horse forward. Four wranglers emerged from the bunkhouse, heading toward one of the barns. He glanced back at the house, close enough now to see the pale curtains over the windows. A road ran under a timbered portal. He followed it into the yard and toward a picket fence. There *was* some grass around the house after all. Ollfinger let his animals graze the place over, but he kept them at arm's length when it came to his living quarters.

Ketcham reined to a stop. "Ollfinger!"

A moment passed before a corner of one of the curtains lifted, then fell back. The door opened and Jeb Ollfinger stepped out onto the little porch, his eyes narrowed, his short-cropped gray hair glowing in the lowering sunlight. His gaze shifted and found Honniger, but his expression never changed. He'd already gotten word that Honniger was dead.

"You've got more brass than a Kansas City saloon, mister, riding here by yourself."

McGruder leaned in the door frame behind him. The son, Thad, lurked in the background.

McGruder came out onto the porch too. "Just like I told you, Mr. Ollfinger. That *farmer* murdered Augie." He put a distasteful spin to the word.

Ketcham ignored him. He'd come here to speak to the older man. "If I remember right, you said you'd keep your boys in line if I came a-visiting."

"That was before you took to shooting my men, Ketcham. There's not much law hereabouts, and I'm prepared to deal with murderers like you on my own terms."

Ketcham gave a small smile and nodded at McGruder. "Is that the way he tells it?"

"It is."

"What you got was a lie . . . again."

McGruder stepped past his boss. "I've taken just about all I'm going to from you." His hand drifted toward the six-shooter on his hip.

"You in a hurry to die, McGruder?" Ketcham said it easy, with a taunting laugh in his voice that only stoked the fire of McGruder's anger. He'd not make a move—not with Ollfinger there. Ketcham's view went back to the owner of the Bar JO, at the same time catching movement to his right. The men who'd gone into the barn had heard them, but it was Ollfinger calling the shots here. They'd make no trouble until he gave the orders. He leaned forward in the saddle. "You either know what's going on and are a damned good liar yourself, or you've been led astray, Ollfinger. I'm guessing you've not got the straight of it from McGruder."

Thad Ollfinger burst from the doorway. "You gonna let him talk to you that way, Pa?"

Ollfinger shouldered in front of his son. "You've got gall, mister."

"Your cows ran a stampede."

"I know that. My men were just heading out now to round them up."

"Did you know they rampaged through the Mattlins' homestead? Tore up their crops? Left them in ruin?"

A glint of surprise flashed briefly in his gray eyes, answering the question. "It's not my fault that old man put his crops down on open range."

"It's not open anymore, Ollfinger. There's a legal deed and bill of sale that went along with that land. Face it, the sodbusters are moving in and you're going to have to make room for them. I'm not saying I like it either, but that's the way it is. Nothing you or your men do is going to stop it. You might run the Mattlins off, but more will come behind them. You can't drive them all off." After he'd said it, he thought it sounded an awful lot like something Margaret Mattlin might say.

Men gathered around, keeping their distance but making it plain he'd not be leaving unless Ollfinger gave the word. Wonderly was among them, standing a little stiff, not moving his right arm much, but outwardly showing no sign of the bullet Ketcham had put in him. He ignored them all. This conversation was between Ollfinger and himself.

"I come here for two reasons, Ollfinger. First, to bring Honniger back. Figured he was your responsibility."

"My respons—"

"Second, when your men round up those runaways, they're going to come up short twenty-two cows. I've got them pastured down on Corely's land. I expect you to draw up a bill of sale for those cows. Consider it part payment for the damage your boys done to the Mattlins' farm today, and the crops they lost."

"Payment!" Rage flared in Ollfinger's eyes and a ruddy tinge crawled up his neck to his ears.

Ketcham eyed the crowd gathered around him. He'd be in a bad way if Ollfinger ever gave the word. He tried not to think of that, bringing his view back to the owner of the Bar JO. "How do you think that stampede got started?" He kept his tone level.

"What are you saying?" Ollfinger's teeth gritted.

"I'm saying that your men sparked those cows a-running. McGruder, Wonderly . . . and Honniger."

McGruder's hand crept nearer his six-shooter. "You better be able to back that up." Maybe he wouldn't wait for Ollfinger to give the word after all.

"Those were the three I saw. He didn't mention Thad. Maybe there were others. Honniger here, he tried to bushwhack me from the ridge. He's dead because he wasn't a very good shot. I guess I was luckier than Hank Mattlin." He added that to see what reaction Ollfinger would give.

Ollfinger didn't give any.

McGruder was on the verge. Ollfinger snagged his arm and stepped between them. "You'd better ride, mister, before I do something you'll regret."

"McGruder and Wonderly tried to jump me afterward. I put a bullet in Wonderly's arm."

"That's a lie!" Wonderly said. "We was pushing those cows to the north pasture just like you told us to, Mr. Ollfinger. That's when this fellow started shooting. He took us by surprise and killed Honniger and got the herd stampeding. That's how it happened." Wonderly took a menacing step toward Ketcham, but his movement was guarded. Ketcham caught the wince of pain in his face that he tried to cover up. Wonderly was hurting bad behind all his bravado. Still, Ketcham must have only grazed him for him to move like that.

"I suppose I cut the barbed wire around Corely Mattlin's crops too."

Ollfinger might have seen Wonderly's pain. If so, he didn't let on. "What's that supposed to mean?"

"It means the wire was down before your men

ran your cows through Corely's crops."

The red crawling up Ollfinger's neck turned bright scarlet. "I've heard enough from you. Get out of here!"

"I'm leaving." His view narrowed toward McGruder. "I sort of understand where your boss is coming from, but I don't know what personal hate burns in you toward the Mattlins. You just see to it you steer clear of their place here on out." His view swung back to Ollfinger. "As for you, Mr. Ollfinger, I'd ask some questions about what's going on here. Start with your son, Thad. I'll wager he can tell you."

"Thad?" Ollfinger glanced at his son, his fists balled into white knuckles. "Get off my land!"

He passed the reins of Honniger's horse to a wrangler. "I'll be expecting that bill of sale made out to Corely, Mr. Ollfinger." He turned his horse, then halted. "Almost forgot. I took this rifle from one of your men the other day. Wouldn't want to be accused of stealing it." Ketcham untied Wonderly's Winchester from his saddle. "I believe it belongs to you." He tossed it hard at Wonderly.

Instinctively Wonderly reached to catch it. He gave out with a groan, clutched his arm, and went to his knees.

Ketcham shifted his view back at Ollfinger. Ollfinger was staring at Wonderly, his mouth dropped open some.

"If you run this place, you better know what's

going on." Turning the mare, Ketcham left them standing there. His shoulders went rigid as he rode away, half expecting a bullet from somewhere, but it didn't come, and he didn't give them the satisfaction of looking back.

Chapter Eleven

Ketcham slept under the stars that night, not wanting to risk bedding down beneath a couple tons of old lumber waiting to crash in on itself. The barn was beyond repair and would have to be torn down and rebuilt. A task bigger than Corely alone could manage.

Come morning he found Margaret bustling about her kitchen, looking purposeful in what she was doing, but somehow distracted. He couldn't determine what was driving her . . . and she wasn't talking. Her farm was in ruin, and no doubt the loss weighed heavy on her, but in spite of all she'd been through, she was busily putting together a basket of food. He didn't ask why, but sipped his coffee and worked at the eggs and fried ham she'd set before him.

The old man sat across the table from him, his round eyes focused on nothing. When Ketcham asked, he said, "Got to get that fence fixed up, then run new furrows."

"Can you bring in another crop this late in the season?"

His eyes drifted back and found Ketcham's face. "Got to, Ketcham. Won't have no money to carry us through the winter if I don't." He grimaced and lowered his gaze, his shoulders slumping. "Who am I fooling, anyway. I know it's too late." He glanced at Margaret's back, then stared at the tabletop. Finally giving in to the truth seemed to wick away whatever vitality was left in him.

"You've got twenty-two head of cows," Ketcham reminded him.

Corely huffed. "What do I know about cows? Anyway, Ollfinger will likely send along men to fetch them back soon enough."

"Maybe. Maybe not." He fell silent.

Margaret's knife hammered the cutting board, demanding attention to itself. Her back was toward them and there was no missing those taut shoulders and that determined stance as she whittled carrots into buttons and scraped them into a pot of boiling water.

"I could drive those cows to the rail line at

Riley's Switch. You'd get a good price at the yards in Chicago."

"Ollfinger would claim I stole 'em from him. And maybe I did. Don't know what the law says about selling another man's beef."

His concern was real. Out of spite, Ollfinger just might accuse him of theft, and in this country Corely would be hard put to prove up his case. It occurred to him just then that staying within the finer points of the law had never been much of a hindrance to what he did. He grimaced and hitched his eyes back to Margaret, presently pulling on padded mittens. If she was listening to their words, she gave no indication of it. She drew a crusty meat pie from the hot oven and the room filled with pleasant aromas that took him back a dozen or more years, sparking memories of the farmhouse where his mother had baked and cared for her family.

His ma and pa had worked their fingers to nubbins making a life for themselves. He didn't appreciate it back then. He never wanted out of life what they had wanted. He'd been young and headstrong, and wild for adventure. The Indians in Arkansas were all tamed, and the land settled and divvied up. There was no adventure there. Leastwise, none that appealed to a sixteen-year-old boy. Farming meant only one thing: tied to the land and rooted there like an old oak tree, condemned to sweat his life away behind a plow and a brace of oxen.

He'd since come to realize that old oaks were sorta like the mountains; they seemed to last forever, solid and dependable.

He had found his adventures while growing to manhood upon the back of a horse, pushing cows, running with hard men, learning to cut his own way through life with fists and guns. He grimaced again. The adventure hadn't turned out to be all it was cracked up to be—at least not the way it had played out in the mind of a boy not quite grown up. There were other things of importance now. Things that smacked of permanence and belonging; unfathomable things beyond the ken of a sixteen-year-old. Oak trees had begun to look good.

He watched Margaret in a way he had not before, admiring the confident way she managed the kitchen and prepared the food baskets. She could manage a house, manage her own life, and be a companion to a man. . . .

He cut off that line of thinking with a sudden urge to saddle his horse and ride to the far horizon, just like that sixteen-year-old boy of long ago.

Corely finished his breakfast, tossing the fork to his plate with a loud clink that brought Ketcham out of his thoughts. "Well, I better go see just how bad it is." He stood, moving a little looser today than the day before. Time, he'd said once before, was all that could heal his bad back, and it seemed to be working.

"I'll go with you."

They walked the fence line down most of its length in back, and much of it in front where the cows had torn through into the yard, making rubble out of the barn. King dashed about the ruined field, stopping here and there to shove his nose into the churned ground and dig with his front paws. A day ago Corely would have driven him out. Today, he let the dog have his way. There was nothing he could hurt any worse than Ollfinger's cows had already done.

Corely stopped from time to time to prop up a lone plant that had escaped a slashing hoof. A careful survey of the field uncovered pockets of green that had not been trampled, mostly near the corners. A strip of sweet potatoes along the north edge had escaped too. Corely was encouraged that at least something of his hard work could be salvaged.

"It ain't much, Ketcham, but there is enough here to get me and Margaret through the winter."

Ketcham shook his head. "Mighty slim pickings."

Corely nodded. "I've survived lean winters before. If Ollfinger thinks he can drive me off this land by a thing like this, whal, then he don't know the meaning of the word *stubborn*."

"I don't think Ollfinger had anything to do with this."

Corely stared at him, suspicion darkening his eyes. "What d'ya mean?"

"I don't think Ollfinger knows all what's been going on."

"You taking his side now? It was his cows what done this. And that man Honniger, he's the one who bushwhacked you."

"I saw the way his men were lying to him. Wonderly and McGruder are behind this, and maybe some of the others. Maybe even his own son. I haven't figured out why, but they're the ones stirring up trouble, then hiding behind Ollfinger, making it look like he's giving the orders."

Corely huffed. "I find that a hard thing to believe, Ketcham."

It did seem incredible. Ollfinger had his reasons for driving Corely and Margaret off the land, but from what Ketcham had seen at the Bar JO headquarters, he didn't figure the man for being ruthless. Ollfinger could have ordered his men to string him up from the hay hoist when he'd brought Honniger's body in. He hadn't. Ollfinger had started this trouble, but it had gone beyond that now. At some point he'd lost control, and he didn't even realize it.

Ketcham shook his head, putting the problem temporarily aside. His view traveled around the field, lingering here and there where the fence still stood. "You'll need to reset the posts and string new wire."

Corely nodded, squinting against the bright morning sunlight. "Got a passel of work ahead of me."

"I'll help you." Stringing wire! What could he be thinking? But the old resistance didn't pull at him as strongly now, and that worried him some.

He looked at Ketcham, his expression unreadable. "You, a cowman man, offering to help a farmer string wire?"

"Don't spread the word."

A lifting twitch at the corner of his mouth was the only expression that showed on Corely's gaunt face. "I won't go and ruin your reputation." Then concern muddied his eyes. "I can't afford to pay you nothing."

"I haven't asked for anything."

A rider came into view on the lane to Corely's house. He was still too far off for Ketcham to see his face, but there was no mistaking the man for his size.

"That's Johnson."

"Pastor Johnson?" Corely squinted into the distance. "Sure enough."

Johnson rode up to the house on his gray Percheron. The big draft animal was meant to be harnessed in front of a freight wagon, rather than saddled and mounted by a single rider. But considering the rider . . .

"Corely. Mr. Ketcham." Johnson reached down and took their hands when they came over. His grip was firm and sincere, his skin rough as pumice stone. The barrel-deep voice said, "Dropped by to see how that back of yours is doing today."

"My back is the least of my troubles, Liam." Corely swung an arm toward the field.

Johnson's eyes narrowed as his gaze swung around and found the sagging barn. "What happened?"

"Ollfinger ran his cows over us."

"Ollfinger did this?"

"Ketcham thinks it was Ollfinger's men who took it on themselves to do the deed. One way or the other, it don't make much difference. It cleaned me out. I'm busted, Liam. It'll be a hard winter."

Johnson's voice softened. "How can I help, Corely?" He dismounted and planted his fists on his hips, peering down at the farmer.

Margaret came out onto the porch. "Pastor Johnson. What brings you out again?"

Johnson turned, sweeping off his hat. "Mrs. Mattlin. Just checking up on Corely. He told me what happened. I'm sorry."

"I am too." Anger rose in her voice. She stiffened a moment before getting it under control.

Margaret would be a force to be reckoned with if she ever once let that deep seething anger get the better of her.

Johnson looked back at Ketcham and Corely, then seemed to remember something. "Oh, Betia has gone into labor. Susan is with her now. She wanted me to let you know."

The storm clouds passed from Margaret's eyes, but her tone was still sharp. "Susan might need

153

my help. I prepared a basket of food for Betia and Ed just this morning. I'll run out there now."

Johnson's smile faltered. "Susan will be pleased to see you."

Margaret went back into the house.

He glanced at Corely and Ketcham. "She's still got that anger to work through."

Ketcham nodded. "It will do her good to go. Get her mind off of this for a while. I'll hitch up the team for her."

"You do that, Ketcham. Me and Liam, we need to talk some." They wandered toward the field.

He gathered the horses out of a small pasture behind the barn and hitched them into their traces. By the time he pulled the wagon around in front of the house, Corely and the preacher were far out in the field, the big man towering over the small, his shoulders bent as if equally bearing the weight of Corely's problem. Corely pointed here and there, while Johnson, his hands thrust deep into the pockets of his trousers, nodded from time to time.

He set the brake on the wagon and stepped up to the porch.

"Come in," she called at his knock. Margaret was at the counter, packing the food she had prepared earlier into two wicker baskets.

"Your wagon's out front."

"Thank you." Her attention remained on the food baskets. That uncomfortable distance between them was back.

154

"Is there anything I can do to help you, Margaret?"

She hesitated, then turned, her eyes purposefully avoiding his. "No, really, Chance. There is nothing." The sudden wooden smile was forced. He sensed a cool determination behind it that set the hairs at the back of his neck on end.

Something had come over Margaret Mattlin in the few minutes it had taken him to bring the wagon around. He wanted to go to her, to put his arms around her and assure her everything was going to be all right. But the distance was real and tangible and . . . impenetrable.

"Really, I've got everything ready. See?" She swept a hand at the baskets.

Maybe it was the stress of losing the crops and barn, and almost their lives? He smiled. "That's a lot of food you've put together there."

"Betia will be bed ridden for many days. Ed needs to keep his strength up." She mirrored his smile, but there was no vitality behind it as she coolly regarded him. He might not have been standing there at all. Her gaze more often than not went past his shoulder and fixed on the wall and door behind him. What was back there that kept capturing her eye?

She laughed lightly. "Really, I'm just fine. Now I need to finish and be on my way. Betia's farm is two miles from here and the morning is already half spent." She smiled, but was clearly impatient for him to leave.

There wasn't anything left to say. "You take care."

"I will. Good-bye, Chance." Her chilling tone was the final brick in the wall that she had erected between them.

He turned, stared a moment at the two closed doors and those tintypes between them, then at Corely's shotgun on the ledge above the outside door. Confused, he left.

Outside, he slanted his steps across the field toward Corely and Johnson. Maybe he had read too much into Margaret's manner? Maybe it was just everything that had happened these last few days—years?—building up inside her. Helping bring new life into the world after all this destruction might just be the medicine she needed to get back on her feet and move on.

He still knew very little about Margaret Mattlin, but he was certain of one thing. She wasn't a quitter. She was a fighter, and this trouble between Ollfinger and the Mattlins still had a good many more rounds to go.

A wrenching thought brought him up short. Could the distance he'd felt be something else altogether? Something that had nothing to do with this trouble? A lump sat heavy in his stomach. After a first infatuation, a smart woman like Margaret Mattlin would see the folly of falling for a man whose feet left only tracks through people's lives. A man who never stopped long enough in one place to build anything permanent. A drifter. A vagabond. A green-pasture wanderer.

Johnson and Corely met him halfway.

"You look like you just lost your best friend, Mr. Ketcham," Johnson said.

"I . . . um, I was just thinking of all the work ahead of us."

"Liam is a-gonna help with the fencing," Corely said, looking more encouraged.

"Many hands make for light work." The preacher's blue eyes glinted in the sunlight as he grinned behind his bushy, black beard.

Ketcham hid his worry. "Good." He welcomed the work—and the help, so long as Johnson didn't fill the hours with his backhanded brand of preaching. The work would do him good too, would take his mind off of Margaret. And when she returned later in the day, he'd see if that wall was still up. If it was, he'd saddle up and move on.

Moving on. The notion lifted his spirits like a drunkard's first sip of red-eye for the day. But like that first drink, a stirring deep inside warned him it wouldn't last.

Chapter Twelve

Margaret stood back from the window, watching them heading for the slanting building that used to be her barn. Corely, bent and still in pain, doggedly led the way. She wished he would take better care of himself, but he knew no limits where his land or his crops were concerned. And what choice did he have now that Hank was gone? She helped with the work as she could, but the place needed another man. Someone young and strong . . .

Then there was Chance Ketcham. She grimaced. Tall and self-assured, how different from her Hank. Hank, like Corely, had loved the land. Unlike Chance, he'd walk five miles out of his way to avoid a fight, not that he couldn't handle himself when there was no way to avoid it. He could. He'd already proved that. But it sometimes drove her crazy the way he would let people take advantage of him.

Oh, Hank . . .

Margaret's eyes brimmed. Angrily, she sleeved away the tears and shifted her view to Pastor Liam, a bear of a man lumbering alongside Corely and Chance. Liam was a contradiction; he was a gentle man on the surface, but sometimes, when he let his guard down, a flint-hard glint would fill his eyes and something like desperation would shadow his face. It made you wonder what he was thinking. What ghosts lived in his closets . . .

As she watched the three of them making their way toward the barn a bitter taste rose in her throat. It hadn't been much to begin with, but now it was rubble! Her gaze fixed there a moment, then returned to the three men, landing on Chance. Her feelings confused her. Hadn't she loved Hank? She had! Desperately so! Then why this growing attraction for a man so different?

She didn't understand it, but she did know that Chance hadn't arrived at their farm by *chance*. He'd been sent to her for a purpose, whether he believed it or not! Her resolve hardened. Any uncertainty she might have harbored earlier vanished. She knew exactly why Mr. Ketcham was here, and she knew what she had to do about it.

She carried the two baskets of food to the table, then hurried to her bedroom, pausing by the door where the tintypes caught her eye. There she was, her face stern, immobilized by the photographer's orders, standing among her family; sepia images of people she'd likely never see again. The second tintype showed her and Hank on the step of the house they left behind in Kansas.

She touched the framed image and blinked moisture from her eyes. Where were those greener pastures now? Hank was dead—murdered! Dorothy too. The farm they thought would satisfy them lay in ruin. Was life here any better than it had been back there?

She retrieved a blanket from atop the chest at the foot of her bed, placed it with the baskets on the table, added a box of matches, and gathered up a crock of water, a lantern, and a small tin can of kerosene. She'd be spending at least one night out-of-doors. She put everything in the wagon except the blanket, which she spread open on the table. In it she carefully rolled Corely's shotgun and the extra box of shotgun shells from the cupboard. Shotgun safely concealed within the blanket, Margaret carried it outside and hid it under the wagon seat.

She was ready. She adjusted her straw bonnet and climbed up onto the wagon. Corely and the others were returning. Corely carried a posthole digger, while Chance and the pastor bore half a dozen fence posts upon their shoulders.

Margaret fixed a smile on her face. "I'm going to the MacRaes' place now. I've fixed a plate of sandwiches for when you men get hungry."

"We'll surely be needing them later." Johnson laughed.

Corely waved. "You take care of yourself now, Margaret."

"I will."

"Tell Susan I'll be here for the day," Johnson said.

"I'll tell her."

Margaret tried to catch Chance's eye, but he kept his gaze averted. Such a peculiar man his moods as fickle as the wind. Her mouth stretched a tight line across her face as she flicked the reins and started away from the farm.

It was a little over two miles east to the MacRae farm. They had six hundred and forty acres, a full section of land, but Ed MacRae had put only about twenty of it into crops. Any more than that was simply too much for one man just getting started to handle. Though small, the house was new, and neatly trimmed with a fresh coat of white paint and a good, solid tin roof overhead. The barn stood straight and strong. The condition of the buildings pulled at Margaret's heart as her wagon rolled up the lane to the house.

Hank had made big plans for fixing up their place. He'd talked almost constantly about re-

Douglas Hirt

building the barn, just as soon as the crops began bringing in enough money for the lumber and hardware.

But it never happened.

She struggled with a bit of jealousy. Betia still had a husband, and soon now would have a child. She reprimanded herself for the uncharitable feelings. Jealousy was not supposed to be a Christian trait. But sadly, it was so much a human one. Revenge wasn't supposed to be a Christian trait either . . .

She quickly smothered that line of thinking. It wasn't revenge. It was justice. Justice that would be found no other way.

Susan Johnson's carriage was there, her horse nipping a broken bale of hay beneath the shade of an ancient mulberry tree. Margaret drew the wagon to a stop. Ed MacRae, standing in the doorway of his barn and reeling in a rope upon his elbow and left hand, smiled and waved when she pulled up. He came over, walking with a rolling gait like a sailor, and helped her down. Ed was a thick-bodied man, not much taller than she, but strong as iron and a tireless worker.

"It is good for ye to come, Mrs. Mattlin." His words bore the remnant of a Scottish accent, which Margaret always found easy to listen to.

"I just heard. How is Betia doing?"

Ed shrugged meaty shoulders beneath the plaid shirt. "I dunna know. I've been banished from me own house." He grinned. "But so far

I've not heard any sounds resembling the cry of a wee bairn. I'll see to your horses. Betia and Mrs. Johnson will be anxious to see ye."

"Thank you." She retrieved the larger of the two baskets from the wagon and went inside. The kitchen and eating area were to the left. A parlor separated them from the bedroom to the right. Betia's small home looked as if she'd just cleaned it for company. The floor, though scrubbed clean as a cat's whisker, was barren of any sort of covering. Ed and Betia had been married only two years and had no extra money to waste on frivolities like rugs and fancy furniture. Everything in the house, Ed had made with his own hands. Betia had sewn all the curtains from old bedsheets and the tail ends of fabric bolts bought from Hawkins at a discount.

Margaret paused in the open doorway to the bedroom. Betia was in bed, knees up and spread, her pale-gray nightgown stretched across her great belly. She had not yet delivered.

Betia's face contorted just then and she let out a low moan. Susan spoke from somewhere on the other side of the bed.

"You're doing fine, Betia. I can see the head." And just then Susan's head popped up over Betia's knees. "Margaret. You're in time."

"What can I do to help?" She swept off her straw bonnet and set it and the basket of food on the handmade table, then went to Betia's side.

Betia managed a fleeting smile that vanished

in a wave of pain and a groan. Her fists bunched in the sheet as her muscles contracted.

"Push again."

"I'm trying!"

Margaret glanced around, spied the bowl with water and a washcloth, and began sponging the sweat streaming from Betia's face.

The pain momentarily lessened and Betia's eyes opened, finding Margaret's face again. "I . . . will . . . never do this again! Men! They start this, but we . . . we women have to finish it! Oowww."

"Push!"

Betia pushed. As far as Margaret could tell, she had little choice in the matter.

Margaret grasped Betia's hand, feeling the uncontrolled strength in it. "It's almost over." How did she know it was almost over? It seemed the thing to say at a time like this.

"Push again . . . okay, we're almost there." Susan appeared to be breathing as hard as Betia.

Betia's face twisted again and a great, long cry escaped her throat. Margaret scrunched her eyes and turned her head, as if that could shut out the agony of the woman's cry.

Then a different cry burst forth in the room. High and demanding, there was no mistaking it.

"You have a son, Betia!"

Betia seemed to collapse within herself, her breathing coming in short gasps. Margaret bathed the sweat from her face and forehead.

"Ten toes, ten fingers, and a healthy set of lungs!"

"Thank God," she whispered, exhausted, but the smile that fell wide across Betia's face shouted her delight.

Susan stood, lovingly cradling the slimy, crying child in her arms.

"He's beautiful," Betia managed.

The door burst open and Ed's voice sounded from the parlor, just outside the bedroom. "Can I come in now?"

"No, you may not." Susan pulled down Betia's nightgown to cover her nakedness. "We are not finished in here yet, Mr. MacRae. But I can tell you, you have a son."

"A laddie!"

"Now, back outside with you," Susan said.

Margaret shooed him out and closed the bedroom door. Susan cut the umbilical and cleaned up mother and child. She swaddled the baby and placed him in Betia's arms.

When they had finished, Margaret went outside and fetched Ed back in. Betia presented her son to his beaming father. "A precious gift," he declared, and strode about the room telling his son what a wonderful life he was going to have. "A true gift from God! I will call him Ian!" He cast a quick glance at Betia with hitched-up eyebrows.

Betia smiled and nodded. "Ian it is."

Ed MacRae tromped around the house again,

naming this and that for Ian, who by this time was fast asleep.

Margaret rescued Ian from his whirlwind tour and shooed Ed from the house again. Betia suckled the child, her face glowing behind a content smile, the torment of only forty-five minutes earlier apparently forgotten.

As mother and child napped, Margaret and Susan sat at the table and shared a pot of tea.

"It's a miracle, isn't it?" Susan spooned honey into her tea and smiled.

She thought she'd heard a wistful note in Susan's voice. A coil of brown hair had worked loose from the bun atop Susan's head and lay in disarray across her brow.

"Yes, it is." She and Hank had tried for just such a *miracle,* but to no avail. And now there would never be that miracle . . . because of one man! The fire rekindled, but she smiled past it at Susan.

"Someday Liam and I hope to have a family."

Susan and Liam had been married six years. Was she to be barren for the rest of her life? A husband, yet no children. Wasn't Susan's plight even worse than her own? "You will." She wanted to sound encouraging, but she was still reining in those unwanted feelings, angry at herself that they had even entered her mind.

I'm not out for revenge. I only want justice done.

"Liam doesn't seem too concerned."

"Oh?" She sensed something more was coming.

"No. He has other worries that occupy him. Children—or the lack of—hasn't started concerning him yet." Susan gave a short laugh. "He's thirty years old. You'd think a man that age would have settled down."

Margaret was surprised to hear he hadn't. "Liam seems rock solid."

"He is in most things." Susan sipped her tea. "But you know what?"

Margaret shook her head.

"I'm not sure he's certain his call to the ministry is the real thing."

"He's a wonderful minister!" Margaret formed a fleeting image of what their church would be like without Liam Johnson in the pulpit. She couldn't hold on to it. "He's not thinking of leaving?"

"Oh, no." Susan frowned. "At least not that he has ever expressed to me."

"Well, you tell him for me he's the finest minister I've ever heard preach. And if he ever even considers leaving, he will have me to answer to."

Susan laughed.

She smiled too, picturing huge Liam Johnson cowering before her threats. "You just tell him he's perfect for the job."

"He'll appreciate hearing that."

The afternoon was still early, and suddenly she was anxious to go, even though the thought of leaving weighed upon her heart. But it was something she had to bear.

"I need to be on my way." She stood.

"Already?" Susan took up the teapot. "Another cup? Surely you have time for that."

"No, thank you. Really, I've . . . things I must see to."

"See you at church Sunday?"

Sunday. Today was Friday. "Of course." She flashed a smile, but her spirit frowned at the lie.

Outside, Ed bounded over. "How are they doing?"

"Betia and Ian are doing fine. Right now they are both asleep, and rest is what they need now."

He frowned. "In other words, back to the barn with ye, Edward."

"Good advice. I'd take it." She smiled. "Oh, by the way, I've left a basket of food on the table. And I'm sure the ladies of the church will see that you're well provided for these next couple weeks. You'll not starve while Betia recovers."

"Thank ye, Mrs. Mattlin. Ye and Corely, well, ye're two of the finest folks I've had the pleasure of knowing." He glanced down. "I just wanted to let ye know."

"We appreciate that, Mr. MacRae." She started for the wagon.

"Ye be leaving us so soon?" Concern flooded his face.

"Don't worry, Mr. MacRae, Susan has everything under control. And I've things I must see to."

He rushed to the wagon and untied the horses for her. "Thank ye for coming."

She climbed up onto the high seat and turned the team away from the house. The wagon rolled slowly down the lane to the main road and stopped. She looked over her shoulder. Ed was standing on the porch, watching her. Her jaw took a firm set. Indecision momentarily fogged her brain. She shook her head as if to clear it.

I'm not out for revenge. I only want justice done.

Resolve replacing the doubt, she turned east onto the main road and clucked her horses forward.

Chapter Thirteen

The first mile was pure misery. A dozen times she drew rein and rethought her decision. A dozen times she almost turned back toward home. A hundred times she told herself it was for justice's sake she was going. And a hundred times she called herself a liar. But by the second mile, if she was not totally comfortable with the lie, she had learned to tolerate it. And after an hour she almost began to believe it.

How long would it be before someone suspected what she'd done? Should she have left a note, just so Corely wouldn't worry? No. Corely would have surely come after her and fetched her back if she had done that. Better that no one knew where she had gone, what she was doing.

It might be hours before anyone suspected she was even missing. So far, everything was working out according to the sketchy plan she had started to devise the moment Chance Ketcham had told her—and he never realized he had.

"Yes, Chance. There was a reason you were sent to me." She grimaced. *Now I'm talking to myself.* She was more agitated than she wanted to admit. What she planned to do frightened her. How could she hope to be successful?

Another hour rolled by. The sun lowered and was warm upon her back, stretching shadows out ahead of her team of horses. Although three or four hours of daylight remained, she should start thinking about finding a place to camp for the night. The notion of camping out in this open country turned a knot in her stomach, but what other choice had she? Again she began to question this trip, and again she firmly put the notion of abandoning it out of her head.

Justice has to be done!

She'd have to find someplace off the road, someplace sheltered where she could build a fire and not worry about being seen.

The land lay mostly flat except for some undulating hills east and north of her. Wildflowers speckled the sere grass with color. They reminded her of the flowers she'd lain upon Hank's and Dorothy's graves, and that reminded her of her mission now. She forced her eyes from the flowers and peered down the road. Someplace up ahead was Riley's Switch. She'd been there two or three times. It was a long way off from the farm—a good day's journey. No chance of reaching it before nightfall.

She worried briefly about highwaymen, though there had been no recent reports of trouble along this road. And Indian troubles were years past. Margaret steeled her nerves and forged ahead. Coyotes, wolves, wildcats . . . they were only a slight concern. She'd lived in the country all her life and knew these hunters rarely bothered humans unless driven by hunger. There was hardly any lack of prey hereabouts. Rabbits and prairie dogs teamed in this land, and quail were abundant.

The plan had taken shape slowly. The main obstacle was getting away on her own. Betia's time coming had been the perfect excuse. Everything was working out. Chance Ketcham's arrival, the word he brought, Betia's baby . . . *I only want justice.*

A brief flicker of red on the road far ahead caught her eye. She stopped the team, staring. Whatever it had been, it had now disappeared beyond the slight rise ahead. It occurred to her just then how very alone she really was. She hadn't seen even one other traveler since beginning her journey.

For maybe three minutes she sat there, then took in a sudden breath and let it out, wishing she could expel the tension in her shoulders and spine as easily. Feeling with a foot under the seat for the shotgun in the blanket, she moved the bundle to the seat beside her and unwrapped it until just a single fold covered the shotgun. Then she flicked the reins and got the team moving again.

"You've got yourself spooked, Margaret." A smile twitched the corners of her mouth. "And you're talking to yourself . . . again."

She drove cautiously toward the crest in the road, and as she rolled over the top and started down, she saw a traveler ahead, small in the distance. He walked in a foot-weary gait, his head hunched forward, a pole slung over his shoulder, its end fastened to a red bundle.

A vagabond . . . a—she searched for the word that was just coming into vogue—a hobo. That's it. She'd not heard good tales about these foot travelers. Was Chance Ketcham such a man? She frowned. Why was he always so near the surface of her brain? She suspected most vagabonds and drifters were men down on their luck and trying to find work, and it was the lazy troublemakers who were giving them a bad name. Somehow, Chance didn't seem to fit the mold.

The wagon drew nearer, and she noticed that this man was shorter than most. A suspicious scowl lowered her eyelids. All at once she was upon him. He hadn't been as far ahead of her as she'd thought. He was only four feet tall!

At the rumble of her wagon the fellow stopped

suddenly and turned. Margaret sat dumbfounded as he peered up at her. He dragged a sleeve of his tattered jacket across his eyes and sniffed.

"Hello," she said.

He stared, his smooth cheeks smudged, a dusty cap pulled down over his shining blue eyes. "Hi," he said after a moment, dropping his gaze to the ground.

Margaret looked around. The road was empty of travelers and there was not another house in sight. "What are you doing out here, all alone?"

"Traveling."

"All by yourself? Where's your mother? Your father?"

His lips tightened, and she thought she detected a tremble. He sniffed again. "I left 'em. And I ain't going back."

"Oh." She was taken aback by the defiance in his voice. "Well, where are you going?"

His small shoulders rolled beneath the light jacket and he pointed up the road.

"What's your name?"

"Henry. Henry Wallace."

Margaret looked around again. It was incredible that this small boy would be out here all alone with no one searching for him.

"Well, hello, Henry. I'm Mrs. Mattlin."

"Ma'am." He nodded politely, then blinked, his eyes losing some of their teary sheen.

Now what was she to do? She couldn't leave a homeless waif on the road. And she certainly didn't need a young boy with her where she was going. She knew herself well enough to realize she wasn't going to leave him. He couldn't have been much older than nine or ten.

"I'm going that way too. Want a ride?" She'd take him as far as Riley's Switch. There'd be someone there who could decide what to do with him.

Henry's expression didn't change, but he nodded. She detected in his guarded willingness a longing for some companionship. He stepped up onto a wheel spoke, grabbed the handrail, and hauled himself up onto the seat. She moved the shotgun back under it.

"You can put your sack back there."

When he straightened around he said, "Where are you going?"

She clucked the horses forward. "Well, first to Riley's Switch, then on to Bailey. How old are you, Henry?"

"Twelve."

She slipped him a suspicious glance. He grimaced and looked away. "I'm really only nine. But I'll be ten in two months."

"Nine years old and all alone." She said it more to herself than for his hearing.

"You all alone too?"

She looked at him. *Alone?* She still had Corely, but in her heart she had been alone since the day Hank died. "Yes, I am all alone, for a little while at least."

175

Douglas Hirt

"Where is your husband?"

She grimaced. "My husband is dead."

"Oh."

It was hard work, and with each post set, Ketcham noted that the shadow it cast was just a little longer. They'd taken a break earlier and eaten the sandwiches Margaret had left for them. At about four o'clock they hovered around the pump, splashing water on their faces and drinking deep of the cold water. That had been two hours ago, and now the day was about spent.

Corely had begun slowing down not long after they started, but Liam Johnson chugged right along like a small steam locomotive, doing the work of four men—driving that posthole digger into the ground and lifting up the dirt, driving and lifting, driving and lifting, moving with the steady rhythm of a machine. In the beginning Ketcham was determined to match the man hole for hole, post for post, but he soon discovered he might as well try to match Hannibal's elephants than Liam Johnson's muscles. The competition had grown old, and there was no joy in a game you could not possibly win.

Now he found himself distracted, his view straying more often toward the lane that led up to the house.

Corely dragged up two fence posts, looking like they weighed a hundred pounds each, and dropped them. He puffed and braced himself

176

against one of the newly set posts. "This is the last of 'em, boys. Tomorrow I'll have to get busy cutting more."

"I'll be by in the morning to help finish this up," Johnson said, not missing a beat with the digger.

"When was Margaret supposed to be back?" Ketcham asked.

The men looked toward the house. Corely lifted his narrow shoulders. "I don't think she said."

"There's no telling." Johnson rammed the digger down and brought up a load of dirt. "Babies don't come by railroad time." He laughed.

"It will be getting dark soon." He shaded his eyes toward the west, where the sun glowed softly through the brilliant green veil of the cottonwood leaves.

"She and Susan will likely come back together," Johnson said.

Corely and Johnson seemed unconcerned, and he figured his worrying was probably not called for either. *Just the same—*

"Someone's coming," Johnson said. Dropping the digger in the hole, he swung around toward the rise of land beyond the farm.

"Recognize him?" Corely squinted.

"Too far off yet."

Ketcham's first thought was of his rifle and revolver back in the house. But here again, neither Corely nor Johnson appeared concerned. He gave a wry grin. He'd been living by wits and fists so long, he'd lost the natural trust men develop living among one another.

The rider neared. Johnson said, "Why, that's Ford Fargo."

"Fargo?" Corely said, surprised. "What does he want here?"

"Who's Ford Fargo?"

Johnson said, "He's the farrier over at the Bar JO. Jeb Ollfinger's place. A friend of mine—ours," he added with a look to Corely. "A church-going man, and one who doesn't pick which side to sit on come Sunday morning."

He recalled Johnson mentioning something about cowmen and farmers keeping to their own side of the church. Ford Fargo loped up to the posthole Johnson had been digging.

"Afternoon, Ford," Corely said.

"Corely. Pastor Johnson." He glanced at Ketcham and nodded a greeting.

For both Johnson and Fargo being in the same line of work, he couldn't have pictured a greater contrast. Ford Fargo was a grizzled fellow of maybe fifty winters. The years of shoeing horses had ruined his back and he sat bent forward in the saddle, making him appear ancient. He had tobacco-stained teeth and drooping brown eyes, and was built along the lines of Corely, with hardly any meat on his frame to speak of. But Ketcham knew that could be deceptive. Wielding a twelve-pound hammer and pumping a forge tended to temper a man's muscles with spring-steel strength.

Fargo's tattered brown Stetson had a cracked brim and was speckled with black burn marks where forge embers had landed on it. His brown vest hung loose from his shoulders and a gray shirt was opened three buttons at the throat. Fargo carried neither a side arm nor a saddle carbine.

Corely took Fargo's outstretched hand. "What brings you out, Ford?"

"Got some news I figured you ought to hear." He shifted his view. "You must be that Ketcham fellow."

Ketcham nodded.

Corely frowned. "What news?"

Fargo spoke to Ketcham. "After you pulled out last night, the boss was spitting mad. He went through the Bar JO like a dust devil through a paper tent. Questioned every man there, me included, then whaled into his son until he got the boy to talking, and when Thad finally did open his mouth, whoo-eee." Fargo shook his head. "Well, once the storm passed and the leaves settled, both Case McGruder and Kit Wonderly had been shown the door."

Johnson gave a low, rumbling chuckle. "He fired those two?"

"Straight enough, he did. Fired them both on the spot. Told them they could stay the night but had to be off his land by noon today."

"That ain't exactly bad news to hear," Corely said, a small smile at his thin lips.

"That depends," Ketcham said. He knew what men like McGruder and Wonderly were like. This sort of thing might send them riding a vengeance trail. "What are they going to do now?"

"That's why I come out to warn you."

Corely's smile faltered.

"What are those two up to?" Johnson's folded arms lay like two lengths of cordwood across his chest, his blue eyes suddenly darker behind his bushy brows.

"You know where my affections lie, Pastor. I'm a man who likes horses, and I like cows. And I like to see them moving free across the land. I never made no bones about that. But you and Corely and me, we are all brothers in another way, and that way runs deeper than cows or fences. You know what I mean, Pastor."

Johnson nodded.

"So I figured I got to tell you."

Ketcham advanced a step. "What is it?"

Fargo shifted back to look at him. "It's like this. This morning I put a new shoe on McGruder's horse. You know, getting the animal fit to travel. I never cared much for McGruder. He's got a mean streak through him that makes a man shiver just to think of what he could and might do. Well, him and Kit, they was fuming at being fired, and being dressed down by the boss. They was talking about getting even. Now, when I heard that, I thought it was Mr. Ollfinger they was talking about, but then McGruder says your name, Corely, and . . . and Mrs. Mattlin's too. And I didn't like the leer in Wonderly's eye when she was mentioned."

Corely groaned and looked around over his shoulder. "They're coming here?"

"I don't know anything for true, Corely. Only what they was saying, and you got to remember they was mad at the time. They said something else, too, something that makes me think maybe they plan on pulling out of the Territory. There was some words about Texas." Fargo shrugged. "So I don't know if they are planning on coming here or not, Corely, but I reckoned you ought to know."

"What's in Texas for them?" Ketcham asked.

"Wonderly's got a cousin who works on a ranch over Bailey way."

Ketcham knew most of the ranches in that part of Texas. At one time or another he'd drifted between jobs on at least a half dozen of them. "What ranch?"

Fargo's eyebrows knitted together, his mouth twisting to one side. "Can't say I recollect which one, Ketcham. He used to work with us out at the Bar JO, but I never had much to do with the man. He was a braggart and a bully. He drank hard and gambled away his nights, and when he wasn't off doing the boss's work, he was making a lot of noise out back of the barn with that six-shooter of his, practicing shooting bottles off a fence rail." Fargo glanced at Corely. "You know him. The fellow who pulled out of here just before your . . . your loss, Corely."

"Oh, him." Corely grunted. "Might have figured that one and Wonderly was kin."

Johnson frowned. "Bad blood runs thick in some families."

Ketcham was beginning to understand. "The man Margaret claims murdered her husband?"

"The very one," Corely said.

It occurred to him that so far nobody had given a name to the man Margaret claimed had murdered her husband and mother-in-law. He recalled her curiosity, her subtle but probing questions, when he'd mentioned he had just come from Bailey. It was beginning to make sense.

"Well, I best be getting back to the ranch. The boss will have my hide if he finds out I let on what happened at his place."

"Understand, Ford." Corely's spirits were mired in worry. "Thanks for letting me know."

Fargo nodded and reined his horse around and rode back the way he had come.

Johnson heaved up his posthole digger and rammed it down hard, giving it a twist and lifting up a load of dirt. "If it isn't one thing, it's another, heh, Corely? Don't let it get you down. Like Ford said, those two yahoos might be halfway to Riley's Switch by now."

"I know." Corely seemed to sag under the weight of this new concern.

Johnson took one more bite out of the earth. "That should do it."

Ketcham hefted a fence post into the hole. "That man who went off to Bailey. What was his name?"

Corely's bony head lifted off his stooped shoulders. "Margaret didn't tell you?"

He shook his head.

"His name was Gellerman."

"Gellerman?" That was a name he hadn't expected to hear. "Benny Gellerman?"

Both men looked at him. Johnson said, "You know the man?"

"Benny Gellerman is one of the reasons I pulled out of Bailey. I skinned him good at a poker table, and he got some men together and went hunting my hide. But I'd already made up my mind to pull out. Him being on the warpath made it seem like a good time to do it."

Just then Susan Johnson's buggy rolled up to the house. "Wonder where Margaret is?" Corely said, squinting down the lane.

Ketcham started across the field, his stomach knotting as he glanced down the lane to the main road, not seeing Margaret's wagon anywhere. Johnson was at his side, matching him stride for stride while a dozen paces behind them Corely hurried to keep up.

Susan smiled as he and Johnson neared the

buggy. "It is a boy. Ian Robert MacRae."

"Where's Margaret?" The urgency in Ketcham's voice dislodged the smile from her face and her eyes rounded.

"She isn't here?"

Johnson's thick eyebrows dipped. "She's not still with Betia?"

"No. Margaret left hours ago."

The knot clenched tighter. "Did she mention she was going someplace else?" Ketcham had a sudden suspicion, and hoped he was wrong.

Corely joined them. "Margaret would have told us so. She'd not just go off and let us worry."

"Mr. MacRae saw Margaret turn east after leaving his farm. He mentioned it briefly, but we didn't think too much of it."

"East?" Ketcham glanced at Corely. "Does she know anyone east of the MacRaes' place?"

"No. Not that I know."

He remembered his long ride from Bailey. "That's the road to Riley's Switch, isn't it?"

"You think she might have gone to Riley's Switch?" Johnson asked.

He shook his head. "I think she might be on her way to Bailey."

Corely stared at him. "Bailey?"

Ketcham bounded up the porch steps and into the house, recalling her preoccupation earlier when he had spoken to her. The shotgun was gone.

"She *has* gone to Bailey, Corely, and she's

taken your shotgun," he said, coming out of the house.

"My shotgun!"

"What makes you think Margaret would be going there?" Johnson asked.

"Fargo just told us. That man, Gellerman, he went to Bailey. That was where he ran to after killing Hank Mattlin."

The preacher frowned. "No one knows for sure it was Gellerman who did it."

"Margaret suspected he did. And with Gellerman gone, and Wonderly and McGruder not talking, she had no way to know where to find him. Then I came into the picture, not knowing what had happened. I mentioned Gellerman's name one day. I remember seeing something change in her eyes. I didn't understand it then. But I do now. Margaret's taken matters into her own hands."

"She must have been planning it for days," Corely said.

"She did seem anxious to leave." Susan bit her lower lip, worry filling her face.

Johnson said, "Would Margaret do such a thing?"

Corely looked confused and shook his head. "I don't know, Liam."

Even if Corely didn't know, Ketcham did. He'd sensed that core of inner determination; there was more to Margaret Mattlin than she cared to let on. She could and she would do such a thing. But just how far she would go to see the man responsible for her husband's death pay for his crime, he didn't know.

"One thing is for certain, someone's got to go after her."

"I'm going with you, Ketcham." Johnson looked at his wife. "You go home, Susan."

She nodded. "I'll be all right. Both of you be careful."

Chapter Fourteen

Long shadows rippled across the land as Ketcham and Johnson rode away from the Mattlin farm. Neither man spoke, and Ketcham fought back the urge to ride hard. The trip could be a long one, and it wouldn't do to wear out their horses at the start of it. Like himself, he figured the big man riding alongside him would be recalling Ford Fargo's warning. McGruder and Wonderly might be anywhere along this road. If those two should come upon Margaret before he and Johnson . . .

A cold shiver tickled Ketcham's spine at the thought of what they might do.

Johnson pointed out the MacRae farm as they rode past the place a half hour later. With evening crouching close to the house, a single light showed from the window.

"She has a five-hour head start," Ketcham said, calculating Margaret's lead by what Susan had told them was the time Margaret had left.

"That would put her ten to fifteen miles this side of Riley's Switch—unless she stopped for some reason." Johnson frowned, his features mostly hidden by the dusky light. "I know what you're thinking, Ketcham."

"What's that?"

"You're worrying about McGruder and Wonderly."

"You heard what Fargo said." Dusk darkened the road ahead of them. His view shifted off the long dark track in the hope of catching the flicker of firelight that might reveal a campsite.

"I heard." There was a pause, then, "You know, the Lord has a way of taking care of his own."

He gave Johnson a pinched look, suspecting another sermon was on its way. He didn't want to hear it. "Maybe, Parson, but for me, I'll put my trust in Sam Colt's equalizer." He patted the revolver in his holster.

The preacher frowned but kept his thoughts to himself. Johnson remained silent. When Ketcham looked over, the big man was staring ahead, his lips moving in silent speech.

* * *

With night thickening around them, Margaret Mattlin turned the wagon off the road and steered the horses around the back of a small bluff, out of sight from the road. Henry helped her unhitch the team and hobbled them. There was grass enough for the horses to graze, and water in a nearby ditch.

"You must be hungry, Henry."

The boy nodded.

"I've food in the basket, and the water crock is still full." She smiled at him. "Help me find something to build a fire with, then we'll eat."

By the failing light they collected sticks and dried cakes of cow manure, and got a small fire burning. The feeble flames did little to drive off the chill, but the flickering light was comforting and kept shadows at arm's length. She hung a blue enameled pot of water over the flames, then opened the food basket. She'd not figured on feeding two mouths, but for tonight at least there would be enough for them both to eat.

Henry was a somber child, and tight-lipped about why he had run away from home. She hadn't pressed him on the matter. Her own concerns had occupied her thoughts to the exclusion of the young lad.

Selfish, that's what I've been—still am.

Henry huddled by the flames, warming his hands, watching the yellow tongues licking at the bottom of the pot of water.

She stared too, questioning her decision to set

out on this quest . . . this mission. By this time Corely would be sick with worry. It was cruel to have left like she'd done. *Selfish*. She had no wish to hurt anyone, only to see Gellerman brought to justice. But how was she to do that? She thought of the shotgun in the wagon and a frown tipped her lips. She knew full well how to use a gun, but not like that—not like she'd have to use it if she confronted Gellerman. Who was she fooling, anyway? She'd neither the stomach nor the skill to face a man like Gellerman.

With a sigh, she unpacked the basket. They ate sandwiches and cold, boiled potatoes, and washed it down with hot tea. Afterward, she opened a jar of canned peaches and stabbed out two slices with a fork. Henry ate as though he hadn't seen a decent meal in days.

"When did you leave home?" she asked as he licked sweet syrup from his fingers.

"Two days ago." He brought the tin cup of tea in both hands to his lips, then wiped his mouth on the sleeve of his threadbare jacket.

"Why did you run away?" She'd decided to test the waters, to see if he was ready to open up to her yet . . . to see how far he'd allow her to pry. Since taking him aboard earlier, they hadn't spoken of any matters deeper than the weather, or more personal than their names—except for her telling him she'd been widowed. About all she had gleaned so far was that Henry spoke with a curious accent, one that made her think of far-away cities and dirty skies.

He didn't answer, but peered into the fire and slid another dry cake of manure onto the bright bed of coals. The flames licking up its sides held his eyes.

Margaret frowned. *Men! They are a close-mouthed lot. Why do some men seem to think running away from a problem is the only solution?* Her sudden anger surprised her, and she realized it was Mr. Ketcham, not Henry, she was thinking of.

It was plain Henry didn't intend to tell her anything. She ought to let the matter drop. It was none of her business anyway. Just as Chance Ketcham's business was his own.

"It wasn't my home." His view remained fixed on the flames, firelight dancing on his cheeks beneath a tangle of hair that fell from his cap and hid his ears.

"Whose home was it?"

"The Grosses'. Friends of my aunt."

"Oh." Margaret shifted upon the blanket where she sat with her back against the hard spokes of the wagon wheel, and adjusted a shawl across her shoulders. "Why were you living with the Grosses?"

"Aunt Theresa . . . died." The small campfire still held his full attention—maybe because he didn't want her to see his face just then. At least she had him talking. She probed a little deeper.

"What of your mother and father, Henry?"

The fire crackled softly as he stirred the embers with a twig. The far-off yipping of a coyote drifted in on the chill night breeze. Margaret hitched the shawl tighter.

"Ma got real sick. We had to go live with Aunt Theresa in Colorado Springs. Pa, he stayed back to work on the docks." Henry shook his head. "Ma had to go to a sanitation, up on Austin's Bluffs."

"A sanatorium?"

"Yeah. A sanatorium. Me, I had to stay with Aunt Theresa." He fell silent.

"What happened then?" she prodded.

He sniffed and brought a finger to his eye. "Ma died in May. Pa, he never come out to the funeral. Never answered no telegrams." Tears choked his voice. "In November, Aunt Theresa got the influenza, and she died too. That's when the Grosses wrote a letter saying they'd take me to live with them on their farm."

"But it didn't work out?"

He was beginning to shiver. "They didn't want no boy of their own. Mr. Grosse, he worked me sunup to sundown. Carried a hickory switch. They was all the time saying how I owed them because they took me in." His lips quivered. "And how my pa abandoned me. And that I must have done something bad for God to punish me so."

He could no longer hold back his tears.

She went to the boy, taking him into her arms. Feeling his sobs against her heart, her eyes brimmed too. How could anyone be so pitiless toward an orphaned child! She pulled the shawl around both of them and leaned back against the hard wheel spoke. He didn't resist her.

"God doesn't punish little children, Henry." Her anger boiled toward people she didn't even know. "Bad things sometimes happen to good people, and there is no explaining why. It's the curse we face every day living in this vale of tears."

His sobbing slowly ceased, but he didn't draw away from her, and she was glad for that. There was comfort in comforting someone else. Somehow, it helped soothe the pain in her own heart. How often she had longed for a child of her own a dream dashed to pieces and scattered when Hank died. But she was still young, although by twenty-five most women had their families well established and their lives plainly laid out before them. Betia was barely twenty, with a son now, and a good husband. . . .

Margaret struck out at the jealousy monster rearing its ugly head again. She refused to go down that road!

As Henry's breathing slowed to an even beat, she contemplated her shattered home and life. Could Corely put it back together? What if he had extra help? Chance Ketcham? A flame flickered and quickened her breath. What was it inside her that drew her to such men? What had she once seen, even innocently, in the likes of Kit Wonderly? Hank had been so very different. Why was she intrigued by men who lived their lives wider and harder than others? Why had Chance Ketcham drawn her like water draws a thirsty deer?

She struck down that line of thinking too. Mr. Ketcham was a drifter. She would not allow herself even idly to consider someone as unsettled as the wind, as . . . as intangible as a shadow. Like Henry, Chance Ketcham was always running away from problems. What she needed in her life was stability and permanence. What she needed was Hank!

She squeezed her eyes and wiped a tear from her cheek. The coyotes were talking tonight; lonely conversation out on the prairie . . . like what she was having with herself. She shifted on the blanket and bunched a corner of the shawl behind her head. In his sleep, Henry snuggled closer. She leaned against the boy and watched the last embers of their fire die against the night.

At first light, Chance Ketcham was up and breaking camp. He shook out his bedroll and brushed off the dry grass clinging to it, then rolled it tight, tied it behind his saddle, and glanced over at Johnson.

"Looks like you're liable to miss church tomorrow, Parson." The sun was just breaking above the eastern hills. He kneaded the place on his back where a rock, hidden beneath his blanket, had worn a sore spot during the night.

"We'll see." Johnson tossed his saddle atop the tall Percheron and threaded the buckles. "If I do, then it was meant to be. Besides, if Margaret has done like you think, I'll be needed here more than there. Susan will tell Ned Wheely, and Ned'll know what to do. My congregation will understand."

Ketcham eyed the charred ring of last night's campfire. A cup of coffee would sit comfortable in his belly about now, but it was no time to be thinking of his own comforts.

"What do you think, Johnson? You know Margaret. Is chasing after Gellerman something she'd likely do?"

Johnson rolled his big shoulders. "I've been questioning this myself. I'd not suspect Margaret to run off and do something like this, but thinking it over some, I'm not all that surprised either. She's a woman with deep feelings, Ketcham. And she keeps them under tight control. You hold back a dam too long and something's going to burst."

Deep feelings. She must have loved her husband fiercely to go off on her own to seek revenge—at least he strongly suspected she had. So far that was all it was. A suspicion. They'd found no solid proof she'd gone after Gellerman. Maybe he and Johnson were on a fool's errand?

He buckled on his gunbelt. Johnson wasn't armed. Big as he was, a bullet would put him down. He hoped it wouldn't come to gunplay. He had to find Margaret before she found Gellerman.

Find her and bring her home.

He grimaced. In some remote way he'd begun to think of it as his home. It wasn't! It was her home. Yet the distinction seemed to have blurred. He slipped his Winchester from its saddle boot. "You ever use one of these, Johnson?"

The big man tugged the girth strap tight and looked over the top of his saddle at him. "A rifle?" He grinned. "I haven't much use for firearms, Ketcham."

"You might want to learn." He tossed him the rifle. Johnson snatched the rifle from the air.

"It's a lever-action repeater."

"Hmm? Is that what it's called?"

"You've got nine bullets in the magazine, one in the chamber. It may come where you'll need to know how to use it."

"Do you really think it will come to that?" He frowned at the rifle, tiny in his fist.

"You never can tell. I'd feel better knowing you were armed." He fished a blackened bean can from the ashes of last night's fire and flung it down the road. "Shoot that. Just sight along the barrel. Put the front sight on the target and center it in the V of the rear sight. Then squeeze back easy on the trigger."

Johnson looked unsure about the exercise. "You really think this is necessary?"

Ketcham slung his saddlebags atop his horse and buckled them in place. "The thing is for you to get familiar with the feel of it. I'd feel a mite better if you had shot one at least once and could hold it like you meant business."

Johnson frowned and moved reluctantly out into the middle of the road. "Front sight on the can. Center it in the rear sight. Pull the trigger?"

"Squeeze the trigger. Pulling it will jerk the rifle off target. There will be a small recoil." He grinned. "But a man your size might not feel it at all."

"Squeeeeze the trigger. I think I understand." Johnson turned, eyed the can a moment, then looked back at Ketcham. "Really, I don't—"

"Go on, give it a try."

"Squeeeeze the trigger." The big man turned back and the rifle leaped to his shoulder and boomed. Down the road, the can kicked into the air. Johnson had cycled the lever by the time the can had bounced back to the road, and he popped it again, then skipped it three more times before lowering the rifle and peering innocently at Ketcham. "Is that the way it's supposed to be done?" He laughed. "Your mouth's sagging a bit, Ketcham."

Ketcham came around his horse and stood in the road, squinting at the punctured can lying almost a hundred yards off. "You weren't always a preacher, were you?"

"Shoot, Ketcham, everyone was something else at one time or another. Who knows, you might have even been a wrangler before you hauled freight." He laughed again, put the rifle in Ketcham's hand, and went back to finish saddling his horse.

Chapter Fifteen

Margaret roused Henry early and hustled him aboard the wagon without even taking the time to heat water for tea. Her determination had wavered during the night. She couldn't take the chance that it would deteriorate further.

Justice must be done!

Her jaw took a firm set and her eyes narrowed with determination. She knew where Mr. Gellerman was now. Nothing must stop her from finishing the job she started out to do.

The wagon rattled on, raising a cloud behind them. There was another concern, too.

She cast a nervous eye over her shoulder.

Sooner or later Corely would come after her.

Hopefully, it would be later. She flicked the reins, increasing her speed slightly.

"New York." Henry's small voice razored through the rhythm of hoofbeats. She looked at him.

He slouched there on the hard seat beside her where she had doubled up the blanket for padding, his short legs stretched out, his scuffed brogans propped on the toeboard. His now-scrubbed pink face looked up at her from beneath the flapping brim of the tattered hat. Something had changed in the boy during the night. He'd awakened in a mood to talk.

"New York?"

"I'm going to find my pa."

"Is that where you lived?"

"Uh-huh."

She struggled to picture a youngster like Henry making such a lengthy trip by himself. "Do you know how far away New York is?"

He shook his head. "A far hike on a hard trail, like Pa used to say. Most of two hundred miles, I suspect."

She laughed. "An apt description, young Mr. Henry. That 'far hike' is most of ten times two hundred miles, and then some, I'll venture to say."

"How much is that?"

"A good deal more than two thousand miles."

He clasped his hat against a side gust of wind and stared at her.

"Have you any money?"

He shook his head. "No, ma'am."

"Then how will you make your far hike?"

"I can ride a train."

"You need a ticket to ride a train. And railroad tickets are expensive."

"I can hide somewhere? I heard a tale about a man who rode under a Pullman parlor car clear across the country."

She speared him with narrowed eyes. "I'll hear no such talk. Hopping trains is dangerous business. You can get yourself killed playing around machines like that. Now, no foolishness about stowing away." She lifted her chin toward the line of buildings coming into view, still small on the horizon. Wind and dust stung her eyes and coated her cheeks and hands, and she longed for a bath and clean clothes. "That must be Riley's Switch."

Henry straightened up in the seat.

"I hear a federal marshal makes it to Riley's Switch on a regular schedule. We'll see if we can find him. He's sure to know of someone to look after you."

She sensed him stiffen. "I ain't going back." It was almost a whisper, but there was no denying the unbendable determination in his words.

She took in an impatient breath and exhaled sharply. What she had to do, she had to do alone. There was no place in her plans for a little boy.

Riley's Switch consisted mainly of a rail siding

201

off the main line and a handful of shacks, most belonging to the Atchison, Topeka & Santa Fe Railroad. The few businesses there catered mainly to the occasional travelers the railroad brought their way. She was amazed such a place could survive at all. Other than some men in greasy overalls who stared at her as she rolled past, the town appeared abandoned. *Town? That's being generous.* If it wasn't for the railroad, Riley's Switch would disperse back into the dusty earth from which it came.

She wondered why someplace like Riley's Switch would be on a marshal's circuit. Maybe it was because of the mining payrolls that regularly rolled through? Would he be here today? She guided the team down the single, rutted track and saw no indication where a marshal might hang his hat.

She spied a watering trough and pulled the team to a stop in front of it. The general store that stood opposite the trough made Hawkins's store back in Carson appear like a grand emporium! She shook her head, recalling Hawkins's often-pronounced claim that he should have set up shop in Riley's Switch.

Men. Never content with where they are!

Were they all the same? Had her Hank secretly longed for the wandering life?

"Let's see if we can find the marshal, Henry."

Reluctantly, he climbed down off the wagon and followed her into the store. The floorboards creaked beneath her feet as she and Henry ventured into a building no larger than her own little house, with half-empty shelves lining the walls. The feeble light through a dingy window made it almost impossible to read the labels. Some items had been shelved so long, cobwebs connected them to the wall behind. No one was inside. Dust lay thick upon the merchandise. Her toe smacked a can of Van Camp's Beans and startled her as it rolled across the floor.

"Doesn't look like anyone is here," she whispered, as if eager not to arouse the attention of anyone who might be.

Henry reached for a box of Arm & Hammer baking soda and looked at the picture.

" 'Ere, put that down, boy, unless you intend to buy it." The gruff voice came from a doorway behind them. She wheeled around. A stocky man emerged from a dark back room. He wore gray trousers and no shirt, only a dirty red union suit, opened at the throat. Heavy-jowled and bald-headed, the man bore an unfriendly scowl as his heavy boots clunked upon the floor.

"Tell your boy to leave that alone. I break the arms of thieves."

"Henry is not a thief." She gathered him to her side and glanced at the box. "Put it back."

The man looked her up and down as if she'd been standing there in the altogether. She cringed beneath his glare. "No trains stopped here in over a day. Where did you come from?"

She regrouped, determined not to be cowed by this man. "We arrived in my wagon."

"Why?"

"And why not?"

A thin smile nudged his thick lips. "Feisty one, ain't you?" He strode past her and stood in the doorway, looking up and down the street. "Where is your man?"

"Henry and I are alone." Immediately she realized the danger in such an admission.

He turned heavily, the thin smile broadening. "Alone, heh? Well, well. What can I do for you?"

"You can provide us with information, thank you. I understand a federal marshal comes through Riley's Switch on a regular schedule. He wouldn't happen to be here today, would he?"

"The marshal?" A frown replaced the grin. "Sure. He's here. Been here all week."

Her tension eased a little. At least there'd be someone she could call if this fellow got forward with her. "Where might I find him?"

He jerked his head at the door. "Across the street. The Pink Garter Saloon." A deep laugh erupted. "It's still early. If you hurry, you might even catch him sober."

"Sober?"

He laughed harder at her surprise.

Firming her grip on Henry's hand, she made for the door, hoping the man would give way for her. He did at the last moment, his rumbling laugh chasing her out into the street. The drab little town seemed almost cheerful compared to the store. She shivered, fighting the urge to flee. Across the street stood a clapboard building, a name painted in rude pink letters. Its door flung open, and sunlight slanting through it showed two or three men standing at a bar.

She hustled Henry back into the wagon and drove out of town.

The string of shacks clustered along either side of the AT&SF tracks came into view a few hours later. Ketcham had had his first view of Riley's Switch coming at it from the other direction. It didn't look much different riding toward it from the west. He hoped to find Margaret there. It gnawed at him that McGruder and Wonderly could be somewhere nearby. He'd kept an eye out for them. Ford Fargo said they might be making their way to Bailey, but so far the only other traveler they'd passed had been a pot peddler driving a noisy wagon. The tinker hadn't seen a woman alone—hadn't seen many wayfarers at all since leaving Amarillo four days earlier.

They rode in among the unpainted, roughboard buildings. In a sweeping glance, he took in the drab place, not seeing any sign of Margaret's wagon. "We'll have to ask around."

"She's not here, I can tell you that." Johnson inclined his shaggy head at the only wagon in sight, a freighter pulled up alongside a toolshed, missing a right front wheel. Three horses stood at a hitching rail in front of a saloon, and a dilapidated delivery cart with a single gray mule in harness stood by a watering trough in front of the general store. They tied up at a saloon called the Pink Garter. Near the tracks eight men were off-loading crates from a flatbed railroad car sitting on a siding.

"Maybe one of them saw her come through," Ketcham said.

Johnson fell in step beside him.

"So, what were you when you were something else?"

Johnson's short laugh rumbled up from his belly. "It took you long enough to ask."

He glanced over and grinned. "If you wanted to tell it so bad, why'd you have to wait to be asked?"

Johnson shrugged. "I don't know. You probably wouldn't believe it if I told you."

"A lie from the mouth of a preacher?" He had a fleeting vision of Dunsbury and the widow, Ethel Grooms.

Johnson gave him a knowing look. "Preachers are just as human as freighters."

Ketcham stopped. "So, what were you?"

"A lawman."

"You're joking."

A smile pushed Johnson's coal-black beard apart. "No. It's true. I, my two brothers, and my father, we were all lawmen."

"Where?"

"Michigan. Detroit."

"Why'd you quit?"

The smile wavered, fading. "I don't know. I felt the call to the ministry. Who can explain the will of God?" Johnson dropped momentarily into silent contemplation. Ketcham sensed something was troubling the big man. "You ever wonder if what you're doing is all wrong, Ketcham? Like maybe you've gone down a path that you should've best left unexplored?"

"That's my life. One wrong path after another. But I figure there's always another trail to ride, and I'll strike upon the right one sooner or later."

Johnson grimaced. "Is that so? You figure the time will ever come when you'll try to untangle all those wrong trails traveled?"

"Is that your life, Pastor? You don't look like a man with tangles."

Johnson winced.

Ketcham wasn't in the habit of giving advice, especially to a preacher. He grasped for something to say. "If your calling was from God, and you truly believe in that sort of thing, then how could it be wrong?"

"That's what Susan keeps telling me. But you know what, Ketcham? I miss it. I really do. It was rewarding work."

They started to walk again. "And preaching isn't?"

A startled look leaped to Johnson's face. "Certainly it is! But in a different way."

He laughed. "Seems to me like you don't know what you want, Preacher." Thinking it over, it really wasn't all that funny. "I reckon you and me, we're more alike than I first thought."

The only worker standing there with his hands free was the one supervising the off-loading. Ketcham asked him if he'd seen a woman come into town earlier.

"Yeah, I seen her. She come through about three hours ago."

"Did she happen to say where she was going?"

"Didn't talk to the lady. But she went into Campbell Osterhouse's place." He pointed to the general store. "Maybe he knows somethin'."

Ketcham and Johnson headed for Osterhouse's store. Just inside the door, Ketcham halted and searched the dim interior. A faint scraping reached his ears from beyond a darkened interior doorway. He stuck his head around it. A stocky man was shoving a crate across the rough floor. "You Osterhouse?"

The man turned slowly and leaned against the crate. "Who the hell wants to know?"

"Chance Ketcham."

"I'm Osterhouse. What do you want?"

"I understand a woman came through here a few hours back. Is it so?" A high, dirty window in the back wall barely let in enough light for Ketcham to see by. Osterhouse was a thickish man in filthy clothes with a big belly and a sweat-slick face.

He came over. "What's it to you? She your woman?"

The man's gruffness set his temper to a slow boil. "She's a friend."

"Friend?" He laughed. "Yeah, your *friend* was here. Kinda purty, that woman. And feisty, too. I wouldn't mind getting friendly with her myself. If you know what I mean. She looked to be able to do a man a real good time."

Ketcham's fist shot out. Osterhouse's arms flung wide, and he staggered into a pile of boxes that tumbled to the floor. Ketcham went for him.

Johnson stepped between them. "We're just trying to find her, mister, not make trouble." He glared at Ketcham, but he spoke to Osterhouse. His words rumbled like distant thunder—far enough away not to be of any immediate worry, but clearly holding the potential of a real gully-washer to come if Osterhouse didn't cooperate. It was a voice that made most men think twice before answering. He gave Ketcham another tight look, then reached down and lifted the stunned Osterhouse to his feet.

Osterhouse glowered at Ketcham, massaging his jaw, but when he spoke his tone had mellowed. "I didn't mean nothing by it."

Why had he struck out at Osterhouse like that?

"The lady stopped to ask a question. That's all. She didn't even buy nothing, just wanted to know if the federal marshal was in town. So I told her."

"Marshal?" Ketcham's eyes narrowed. What would Margaret want with a federal marshal? "Where is this marshal?"

Osterhouse gave a snort. "Where he usually is. The Pink Garter Saloon. Gettin' oiled up."

Johnson said, "And that was all she said?"

"She wasn't real talkative. She just took hold of that son of hers and left."

"Son?" He shot Johnson a glance. The big man gave a barely perceptible shake of his head. "Where is the Pink Garter?"

"Across the street."

They started for the door.

"But you won't learn anything there."

Ketcham swung back. "Why?"

"Because she never got that far. She just loaded her boy onto their wagon and they drove off."

They strode back to their horses.

"Kinda lost control, didn't you, Chance? Fisticuffs with the local citizenry is no way to get folks to cooperate with us."

"I don't know why I did it."

"You don't?" Johnson grunted.

Has she gotten that deeply under my skin? He turned and peered hard at the big man. "We might be following the wrong trail, Johnson. You heard him. That woman had a son." He considered the other thing Osterhouse had told them.

"You were a lawman. Would a federal marshal have jurisdiction in Texas?"

"I don't know about that, but if she is going after Gellerman thinking he killed Hank, then it makes sense. That crime took place in New Mexico Territory. A federal marshal *would* have jurisdiction in that case."

He didn't like the puzzle Osterhouse had given them. It chafed that they were no closer to finding Margaret than they had been yesterday afternoon. "But that woman was traveling with a son?"

"It doesn't make much sense, does it?" Johnson said.

"Unless she isn't Margaret."

Johnson scowled. "You think maybe we jumped the gun. Margaret might be back home right now thinking how foolish we were to fly off the handle."

"I was so sure we'd pick up her trail here." His quick glance took in the little railroad camp again, frustration tightening his fist.

"What do you want to do?"

He wasn't sure. The preacher might be right, but his gut feeling was to press on. "I'm going on to Bailey. You can head home if you want. If you leave now, you can be back in Carson in time for your services tomorrow."

"No, sir, you're stuck with me until we see the end of this here trail, Ketcham."

They mounted up and left Riley's Switch.

Chapter Sixteen

Margaret couldn't put Riley's Switch behind her fast enough. It had been no place to leave a boy, marshal or not. An hour later she passed over the border into Texas, and the United States.

Nothing had really changed, crossing that imaginary line that existed only on maps and legal documents. The land was just as flat and dry and dusty, but something about being back in the States helped sooth her nerves. A mile farther on, a rutted track bent off the main road. A faded sign pointed to the south.

Bailey 20 miles

Her heart seized. This was it, the last leg of her journey. With a grimace, she swallowed down a hard lump and turned onto that track.

"Why are you going to Bailey?" Henry asked as the wagon jostled and bumped along.

"I've business to see to."

"What business?"

"Never you mind."

He recoiled at her sharp reply. She ignored the pang in her heart. Now was not the time to soften.

The shadows alongside the wagon had disappeared. It was almost noon. With these rough roads, it would be hours yet before they reached the town. That couldn't be helped. If she pushed too hard, she might break a wheel!

For the next few hours Henry remained introspectively silent, clutching the iron handhold against the bucking of the wagon.

It was midafternoon when the riders came into view and she pulled to a sudden stop.

"What?" he asked, jarred from his thoughts.

"Some men coming this way, up ahead." If one of them was Gellerman . . .

She felt under the seat for the shotgun that had slid back against the wagon box and moved it to within easy reach.

Henry's eyes rounded at the gun at their feet, then up at her. "Who are they?"

"I don't know yet." She gave the horses a cluck and started them moving. Closer now, she could see the men's faces and started breathing a little easier. Gellerman wasn't one of them. They weren't men she recognized. She was still nervous, but as the riders neared they merely turned their horses off the road to let her pass.

"Ma'am," one of them greeted in passing, giving a respectful nod. He was the taller of the two, his mouth a tight slash cut into his sunburned face. The leathery skin of his gaunt cheeks was carved into deep, weathered folds, but his gray eyes smiled at her.

"*Señora,*" the other said, a Mexican who was shorter and thicker than his friend. He tipped his broad Mexican sombrero with a flourish. "You're a long way from nowhere." Crooked teeth emerged from behind a magnificent mustache.

The gaunt-faced man reined to a stop, his glance taking in her and Henry. "Everything all right, ma'am?"

Maybe he saw the tension in her face. "Yes."

"You and *el jovencito,* you are in no distress, heh?" The Mexican glanced at the brassy sky, shading his eyes with the big hat.

"No. We are fine, thank you."

The tall man nodded, and the Mexican levered his hat back upon his head. They turned to resume their journey.

"How far is it to Bailey?"

The tall one reined back around. "About five or six miles. Maybe another hour in that rig." His gray eyes narrowed with concern. "You meeting someone there?"

"Yes . . . yes, I am." That was stretching the truth some, but it wasn't an out-and-out lie, either.

"Good." The eyes smiled again. "Bailey can be a rough place for a woman on her own. This being Saturday, you're gonna have men in off the range whooping it up, and they can be a rough lot. Best to keep out of their way."

"I will. Thank you."

"You and your boy take care." He and the Mexican rode off, swinging back onto the track.

She fetched up the crock of water, and they each took a long drink from it before she got the team moving again.

"Who are you meeting?" Henry asked.

Throughout the long ride since leaving Riley's Switch, she'd had time to think it through. She'd known the truth from the start. She could never confront a man like Gellerman. No matter how sincerely she tried to deceive herself into thinking she could, deep down inside she never really believed it. There was another way to handle this. The proper way.

"I'm going to meet with the sheriff, Henry." Maybe her resolve had weakened during the night, or maybe it was a good dose of common sense setting in. So long as Gellerman was brought to justice, did it really matter by whose hand it came?

"Why?"

"Because there is a man there who did something very bad, and he must be punished."

"Oh." Henry squirmed on the seat. Maybe he was thinking of Mr. Grosse and his hickory switch.

Leaving the shabby railroad camp, Ketcham brooded over what had happened. It wasn't like him to strike out like that, but the very thought of Osterhouse's lewd suggestions toward Margaret had triggered something in him. Something he didn't fully understand, and wasn't sure he wanted to.

They pushed on eastward and crossed over into Texas. Johnson said, "Could Osterhouse have been mistaken? I mean, about the boy."

He'd wondered the same thing—had wondered and had rejected it. "Not likely. Osterhouse said they both rode away together."

Johnson considered a moment. "You know, Ketcham, sometimes things aren't the way they appear to be."

Was there something deeper buried in that cliché, or was Johnson just looking for words to say? Did Johnson suspect his growing feelings toward Margaret? Did he know something of Margaret's feeling toward him? He grimaced. Why was he always suspicious of the man's intention? If he hardly understood his own feel-

ings, how could Johnson know anything of
them?

The sight of two riders on the road ahead of
them jerked him from his thoughts.

"I see 'em," Johnson said.

They were still far off, but something in the
way they sat their horses eased his concern. It
wasn't McGruder or Wonderly. One was tall and
slender, with hollow cheeks and a stern mouth.
The other was a heavyset Mexican who vaguely
reminded him of his friend Jorge Rodriguez.

They stopped and talked, as travelers looking
for news ahead might.

Ketcham asked if they'd seen a woman. They
had. They'd spoken to her. The description they
gave could have fit most any woman of Margaret's build. "She and her son were heading to
Bailey. Meeting someone there. I figured it was
her husband," the taller one said. He narrowed
an eye at Ketcham. "Just what's your business
with this woman?"

He could hardly blame his suspicion. He'd be
wary of a couple men following a lone woman
on a remote road, too. "She's a friend." But he
was almost certain this woman who'd passed
through Riley's Switch, and now had shown up
on the Bailey road, was not Margaret. *A son?* It
had to be someone else. They'd wasted a day running down a false trail. His mind raced ahead,
trying to guess where Margaret might have gone.
Maybe Johnson was right and they'd jumped the

gun. She could be almost anywhere . . . likely safely at home thinking he and Johnson foolish for chasing off at half-cocked.

"I'm her pastor," Johnson said. "We're concerned about her traveling alone."

Ketcham said, "But the woman you described must be someone else. Margaret has no children, and her husband is dead. I'm afraid we've taken ourselves on a wild chase."

The man nodded as if sensing his disappointment. "Good luck in finding your friend. I hope she doesn't get herself into any trouble."

"*Sí, señors.* I, too, wish you much good luck locating the *señora.*"

Ketcham thanked them, and he and Johnson rode on. It was time to reconsider their journey. There'd been no hard evidence so far that Margaret had made this trip, yet he'd been so certain at the start.

Much larger than Riley's Switch, or even Carson, Bailey was a fair-size town of maybe three or four hundred people. But Carson was home, and Margaret's heart longed to be back there.

"Is this Bailey?" Henry asked.

"This is Bailey." Her chest tightened as the wagon rolled slowly past a hardware store on her left and a livery to her right. She searched for the sheriff's office to no avail: the Cattle King Saloon, Meyer's Meat Market, Wilson's Dry Goods and Clothing, Anson & Kenyon Saloon featuring

Zang's Beer, and Mildred's Restaurant, but no sheriff. What if Bailey's representative of law and order conducted business out of the local saloon like the marshal back in Riley's Switch?

She rejected that notion. It was impossible that could happen twice. She'd just missed it, that's all.

"Henry. Did you see the sheriff's office?"

"No, ma'am."

"Keep looking."

She rolled past a narrow building sandwiched between a bakery and a laundry. A sign—PHILIP MARSTEN, ATTORNEY-AT-LAW—caught her eye and she pulled to a stop in front of the building. She would ask directions, hopefully with better results than in Riley's Switch.

Henry scrambled off the wagon and followed her inside. Mr. Marsten was rocked back in his chair, his feet propped up on a cluttered desk, snoring peacefully when she entered. She closed the door quietly, approached the sleeping man cautiously, and cleared her throat.

Philip Marsten startled awake. Seeing her standing there, he straightened around and stood, grabbing a pair of spectacles off a pile of papers at the corner of the desk. "Good afternoon, ma'am." He extended a hand. "Please excuse me, but I was just catnapping." His black hair, streaked in silver, was tousled, but his smile gleamed at her. In spite of the cluttered desk, Mr.

219

Marsten didn't appear to be a man with an awful lot to do.

"I was hoping you could help me," she began. Mr. Marsten leaped in before she could finish.

"My business is helping people. Title searches, wills, criminal law, anything that has to do with the intricacies of our legal system, I'm your man, Mrs. . . . ?"

"Mattlin. Margaret Mattlin."

"P. D. Marsten, at your service." He straightened his crooked tie and collar, and shoved fingers through his hair.

She smiled. "I don't really need your services as a lawyer, Mr. Marsten."

"Oh?"

"No. I just stopped in to ask directions to—"

"Directions?"

"Yes."

"I see." The smile vanished and Mr. Marsten sat in the chair.

"I'm looking for the local sheriff, but can't seem to find an office anywhere."

Sheriff Hawthorn has an office on B Street. First Street is one block north of here. B Street will be two blocks east."

"Thank you."

"You're welcome. Good day, ma'am." Mr. Marsten pretended to be busy shuffling papers.

She took Henry's hand and returned to the wagon. They found the sheriff's office right where Mr. Marsten said it would be, with a handwritten notice in the window saying Hawthorn would be back tomorrow.

"We're not having a very successful day, are we, Henry?" She frowned at the late-afternoon sky. "I wonder what kind of accommodations they have here in Bailey?" Accommodations were going to cost money, and she and Corely hardly had enough for her to spend it frivolously. Would a room and bed to sleep in be considered frivolous?

"I'm hungry."

She looked at him. "I am too, Henry." She opened her handbag and counted the coins in her purse. It pained her to dip into them, knowing the tough time that lay ahead now that their crop had been destroyed. But wasn't food necessary too? She hadn't planned on feeding two mouths. "I saw a restaurant when we came into town." She set the bag aside and grabbed up the reins.

The wide street where she turned the wagon was nearly empty, but far out across the sere grass prairie that rolled away from the last buildings, she spied maybe half a dozen riders loping toward town. The cowboys that gaunt stranger had warned her about, no doubt. She started back to the main street. Those range riders would likely be heading for one of the many saloons she'd noted coming into town, not for a restaurant.

Mildred's Restaurant was a tinder-dry shack, a fire waiting to happen. She hoped the inevitable blaze would be delayed long enough for her and Henry to eat their dinner. The owner was a woman on in years, maybe fifty, maybe sixty, Margaret couldn't tell. Mildred was a tall woman with a gray face and hollow cheeks, and walked with the help of a cane.

She'd pointed them to a table and recited the fare for the day. Margaret ordered one meal and asked for two plates. Mildred scribbled it down and hobbled back to the kitchen.

While they waited for their food, Mildred thumped from table to table, leaning on a gnarled walking stick as she filled coffee cups from the big, battered black pot. Her apron might have served as the menu of the day.

She had a helper, a thick woman with strands of dark hair lolling across her eyes, puffing cheeks, and a hint of a mustache above her sweaty lip. She wore an apron as telling as Mildred's, and spent most of her time bustling from kitchen to eating area with a serving tray balanced upon a hand and shoulder, breathing hard and clanking plates.

Margaret leaned close to Henry's ear. "It must be dinnertime. They're very busy." Among the smattering of cowboys who would rather eat than drink, there were men who appeared to be shop owners, and others of a more professional nature. She looked for Mr. Marsten, but he wasn't one of them.

"The best places to eat are thems what are the

busiest." Henry said it like it was an established fact, like gravity pulling a rock to earth or fire giving forth warmth.

Margaret's mouth tightened, then she smiled gently. "You miss him terribly, don't you?"

Henry looked at her, biting his lower lip, fighting the tears.

"What is your father's name?"

"Walter Wallace."

She covered his hand with her own. "I'm sure if he could have, he would've come for you, Henry." She glanced to the window as a band of wranglers thumped past on the boardwalk outside. Their ringing spurs and loud voices penetrated the restaurant as if the walls had been canvas.

"Maybe he didn't get word?" Henry said.

She looked back. It was possible, but was it likely? "Maybe. We can send another telegram if you like. There'd be a telegrapher at Riley's Switch. And there's other places too." She didn't recall seeing any wires running into Bailey, but most every town with a depot or siding along the Atchison, Topeka & Santa Fe right-of-way had a telegrapher.

The heavy woman slammed through the back door and came snaking around tables, bearing dinner plates upon the tray on her shoulder. She trundled up to Margaret and Henry's table, dropped the food and extra plate in front of them, and with a single, well-practiced swipe of her fist, slammed salt and pepper shakers onto the table.

"Eat up."

Margaret was struck breathless by the swiftness of the delivery and the speediness at which the woman charged back through the kitchen door.

She carefully divided the food between the two plates.

Henry stared wonderingly at the meager pile in front of him. "What is it?"

"Roast beef and potatoes, I think. At least, that's what we ordered." She moved the food around with her fork just to be sure, then tasted it, and was pleasantly surprised. "Well, it certainly tastes better than it looks."

"It's good?"

"It's very good."

Henry sampled the fare and dug in with a vengeance. Mildred came over with coffee for Margaret. She offered some to Henry, but he shook his head and grabbed for the glass of water instead.

"Is there a hotel in town?" Margaret asked.

"Naw. No hotel here, deary."

"Where do travelers lodge?"

"Travelers don't generally come through Bailey." Mildred laughed as if that was a private joke among the citizens of Bailey. "But Francis Kettering off A Street, she's got rooms she lets by the day or week."

"Kettering?"

"Can't miss her place. Just take A all the way to the end. Francis's house has a porch and rose-bushes out front. Got red flowers blooming. I saw 'em this morning."

"Red roses. End of A Street."

"That's it, deary."

"Thank you."

"You and your boy passing through?"

Margaret glanced at Henry, who was sopping up gravy with a slice of bread. "We'll only be staying the night." She didn't figure it would do to announce the nature of her business.

The older woman eyed her suspiciously. Margaret gave her a quick smile. She'd done smarter things in her life than to go off after a murderer all on her own. "We hope to be going home tomorrow."

Mildred kept her thoughts to herself and hobbled off, coffeepot in one hand, cane in the other.

"We'll go see this Francis Kettering as soon as we leave here."

Henry nodded.

She sipped her coffee. She heard thumping on the boardwalk outside again, and men's voices growing louder. All at once the thumping and voices went silent. She glanced over the rim of her coffee cup at the window. Her breath caught and she gave a startled gasp as her eyes rounded.

On the other side of the glass, Case McGruder, Kit Wonderly, and Benny Gellerman were staring in at her.

225

Chapter Seventeen

Johnson seemed distracted, and fell further behind as his view focused more often than not on the road. At the Bailey turnoff Ketcham drew rein, fished tobacco and paper from his vest pocket, and rolled himself a cigarette, waiting for the preacher to catch up.

He offered him his fixings, when the big man pulled to a halt beside him. Johnson shook his head. Ketcham struck a match, drew the smoke into his lungs, and blew it out in a sharp, impatient breath. "Time we talk this over."

"Let me guess. You don't think Margaret is heading for Bailey, after all?"

"I was certain of it yesterday. Today . . . ?" He shrugged.

"Where else could she have gone?"

"Liberty . . . Brownhorn . . . Fort   Sumner? You tell me, Pastor. She could be anywhere out here, anywhere or nowhere."

"Fixing on trying another direction?"

"Someone would have seen her if she'd come this way."

Johnson frowned. "Would seem that way."

"What's north of here?"

"Not much." The preacher dropped his view to the road again.

"West?"

"Fort Sumner. Carson."

"Carson! Of course." He twisted around in the saddle, peering down the road they'd just traveled as if it were possible to see all the way back to Carson. "That must be it. She didn't go back to the farm because she went to Carson instead."

Margaret gave a startled gasp and immediately glanced away, hoping they hadn't recognized her.

"What's wrong?" Henry asked.

Her heart drummed, blood pounding in her ears. How could she have been so wrong about herself? She'd been a fool to think she could go through with it! Here was the very man she had come all this way to find, yet at the first sight of him her courage sucked dry like water on parched ground. She forced her breathing back to something approaching normal, gulped down the lump in her throat, and whispered, "Those men at the window."

Henry looked over.

"No, don't! You'll draw their attention."

"What men?" Henry's confused gaze returned to her.

She dared not look again. "They're not there?"

He shook his head.

She was frozen with fear, and her head didn't want to move. She forced herself to look anyway. They *were* gone. Gellerman, McGruder, Wonderly . . . had she only imagined them there? No, she was certain of what she had seen. Her heart's wild beat confirmed it. Her eyes darted toward the door. The sidewalk beyond the window was empty. They really had gone!

"Come on."

"I'm not finished."

"We need to go now."

Henry shoveled another forkful of food into his mouth as she fumbled coins from her purse and left the money on the table. She pulled him by the hand toward the door, her heart pounding like a stampede. Fear of what she'd find outside momentarily stayed her hand.

Get a grip on yourself, Margaret. They're gone. They've found their way into some saloon and never really saw you after all.

She opened the door and marched straight to the wagon, not daring to take her eyes from her destination. As she climbed to the seat, an icy finger pierced her spine. With stiff caution, she finally allowed herself to look around. Of the dozen or so men along the boardwalk, none was the three she'd just seen. Someone in the crowd hooted at her and invited her to come with him to the saloon. His friends laughed. She pretended not to hear and turned the wagon. The town became an indistinct blur beyond the corners of her eyes as she started away, concentrating only on the directions to the boardinghouse Mildred had given her.

She drew the shotgun from under the seat and laid it between her and Henry, but there was no comfort in it as there had been the day before. She'd been so confident while hatching this scheme. How could such raw courage—such bravado so carefully kindled and nurtured—so swiftly melt away?

She was disgusted with herself. She'd come to Bailey to see justice done. The goal was noble, her unexpected panic shameful! "I won't let them, Henry! I won't cower and I won't be driven off."

He blinked at her. If her outburst had confused him, he didn't ask. "I didn't see anyone."

"Well, I did."

"The bad man?"

"*Three* bad men, Henry." She turned left onto Third Street and aimed the wagon for the intersection ahead. *A Street all the way to the end. A porch and rosebushes. Red flowers blooming.*

The cold finger screwed deeper into her back-bone and kept her eyes in constant motion. She half expected Mr. McGruder or Kit Wonderly or Mr. Gellerman to leap from some darkened doorway.

But no one did.

Reaching the corner of Third and A Street without incident was a milestone, yet it brought only a margin of relief. She made the turn and searched the doorways and shadowed places between buildings as she rolled past.

You're working yourself into a frenzy. Get control, Margaret. She forced her breathing to come naturally.

The saloons and merchants petered out, giving way to more practical services: a harness-repair shop, an undertaker's parlor, a gravestone cutter, and a large smithy with two forges. Across the street on her left loomed a tall livery stable, with corrals marching right up to the edge of the street. Its big door was open, but the sun was in the wrong place; the building's cavernous interior seemed to snarl at her through the gaping, black maw as she drove past.

Henry swiveled on the seat and watched the other side of the street. Farther down, beyond all the businesses, stood a few homes. They each had a porch, but only one had rosebushes.

"There." She pulled to a stop in front of the neatly trimmed hedge of rosebushes that clearly had been planted to mark the boundary between property and street. A brick walkway led up to the porch.

She looked around. An older man across the way puttered in his yard; a woman three houses up scrubbed windows. Somewhere a door squeaked and a child laughed. She drew in a deep breath and let it out. Normal sounds and sights.

The squeezing in her chest eased and her breathing became more regular. "Well, let's see if we can't get a room for the night." She lighted from the wagon. Henry came around to her side and she dropped a hand to his shoulder. He didn't seem to mind the growing closeness. Just having him along had made the trip easier. How would it have been without him? She couldn't imagine it now. Her fingers tightened ever so slightly on the boy's thin shoulder.

The porch was narrow, painted gray, and scuffed to bare wood near the door. At Margaret's knock, a tall, white-haired woman with a sharp nose appeared in the doorway. Her eyebrows pinched together in a suspicious scowl.

"Yes?"

"I'm looking for Francis Kettering."

"I am she."

Margaret smiled. "My name is Margaret Mattlin. And this is Henry. We were told you might have a room we could let for the night."

"I might. Who sent you to me?"

"The woman at the restaurant."

The scowl eased. "Mildred?"

"Yes."

She considered Margaret and Henry, then stepped back, holding the door open for them. "How long would you and your son be staying?"

"Just tonight. I hope to be going home tomorrow."

"You two alone?" She looked at the wagon, and the scowl thickened again.

"Yes. I'm . . ." It still pained her to say the word. "I'm a widow."

Francis's expression softened, some of her iciness melting. "I'm a widow too." She reached out and touched Margaret's arm. "You can never be too careful, you know." Her eyes darted to the open door as if to say the world out there was a dangerous place. Margaret already knew that.

"I have a room you and your boy can have tonight." She turned to Henry. "Poor lad." She lightly patted his head.

Henry shrank from her touch.

Francis smiled, but the scowl lines remained, as if stamped there by years of living alone.

Is this what I'll look like someday? She'd never considered a time when she would be completely alone, but Corely was old, and . . . She refused to contemplate such a future. A hollowness expanded in her heart. Chance Ketcham's face suddenly filled that empty place. But Chance wasn't permanent. He was a vapor, a drifter passing through her life as he must have so many other women's lives. Henry squirmed beneath her grip.

"Come this way." Francis led them through the parlor and down a hall to a door at the very end. The room was small but clean, with a single bed and a night table holding a lamp, a pitcher, and a china basin. An armoire stood against one wall. A window looked out onto a side yard at a hedge running between Francis's house and the house next door.

"Will this do?"

"It's fine, thank you."

Francis folded her hands in front of her. "The room is eighty cents for the night."

"Eighty cents?" She and Corely could eat all week on eighty cents!

"Dinner is included, of course."

"Of course." The payment sounded expensive, but under the circumstances, probably fair. Her alternative was to sleep out under the stars again, and she didn't relish that thought with Mr. McGruder, Kit Wonderly, and Mr. Gellerman out there somewhere. Reluctantly, she agreed to the charges. The promise of dinner helped lessen the sting somewhat. This venture was costing her more than she'd reckoned. She drew in a sigh of resignation and counted out the coins into Francis's hand.

With a smile, the older lady slipped them into the pocket of her housedress. "You'll want to wash up. I've a pot of hot water on the stove."

Francis retrieved the pitcher from the night table and retreated up the hallway.

Margaret looked around, removing her straw hat. She tested the firmness of the bed with a hand. "It looks clean." She sat on the edge of the bed, pulling back an edge of the bedspread for a peek at the sheets.

"How would you feel about sharing?"

He shrugged.

"We can make a bed for you on the floor, if you'd rather."

"That'll be okay." He hesitated. "Why did she call me your son?"

"Well, she just assumed that you were, that's all."

"Why didn't you tell her I'm not?" He circled the bed and stared out the window.

"Does it bother you she thinks you're my son?"

Henry thought a moment and slowly shook his head.

She smiled. "It didn't bother me either. Besides, if I had told her, we would have had to explain why you were running away. It would have . . . complicated matters."

"You didn't tell the man back in Riley's Switch either, or those two on the road."

"No, I didn't. Maybe I should have. But it felt nice to have a son, even if it was only for pretend. You ever pretend, Henry?"

"Oh, sure." He left the window and climbed up on the edge of the bed beside her. "I pretend a lot. Sometimes I pretend I'm an Indian. Or a pirate. Sometimes I pretend I'm the engineer on a train." His voice trailed off. "Sometimes I pretend my mama is still alive."

Her heart wrenched.

"She used to let me sit on her lap, and she'd read to me from books." He stared at the toes of his scuffed shoes.

"What kind of books?"

"All kinds." His eyes rounded, the sadness leaving his voice. "She read me once about a boy named Pip who was poor and lived in England, and another time about another poor boy named Huckleberry who lived on a big log raft!"

"Really?"

He nodded. "She read a book 'bout a man who traveled under the water in a big iron boat. But the one I remember best was a story about a pirate by the name of Long John Silver who saved a boy named Jim from some bad pirates while hunting for buried treasure! That was the best one of all."

"My! Such exciting stories."

He grinned. "Mostly when I pretend, I pretend I'm a pirate sailing the Spanish Rain."

"Spanish Rain?" Margaret laughed.

Footsteps sounded in the hallway.

"You can tell me all about pirates later."

Francis left the pitcher of hot water, a bar of lavender soap, and two towels.

Margaret and Henry got down to the business

235

of scrubbing away the dust and grime of the road. Afterward, she checked herself in the mirror above the night table. The exercise had much improved their appearances, and their moods.

Chapter Eighteen

When she and Henry finally left their room, the sun was low in the sky, casting long shadows across the street. The wonderful aroma wafting into the parlor from the back of the house reminded her just how hungry she was—even more so now since she'd fled the restaurant, leaving most of her meager dinner sitting on the plate.

Francis came from the kitchen, wiping her hands on her apron; her smile was somehow at odds with the deep lines incised upon her face. "Dinner'll be in forty-five minutes. I've two other guests joining us. Elsie's a dear lady who's just arrived from Hale City. She's to be our next schoolteacher." Francis bent an eye toward Henry. "Do you like school?"

"No."

She frowned.

"And the other?" Margaret asked.

"Jacob Williamson. He's an older man. Eyes are going dim, so he doesn't see too well anymore. Used to be a watchmaker, so he tells it, but nowadays he just sits up in his room playing checkers against himself."

"Oh? Poor man."

Francis shrugged. "He claims now he's finally winning."

She couldn't tell if Francis was joking. If so, the older woman never cracked a smile. Margaret looked out the window at the wagon, and the horses still in harness. "I must take them to the livery stable. They'll need grain and rest for the trip home." She looked at Henry. "You may stay here if you like."

"I'm goin' with you." Henry fidgeted in Francis's presence.

She drove the wagon through the gate and rolled up to the big, open door. It was even darker inside than when she'd passed it the first time. Here and there a smoky lantern cast its feeble light against rough-cut timbers or the dirt floor. The rafters high overhead were completely lost in shadows.

She set the brake and stepped inside. "Hello?"

The muffled sounds of animals came from a

dim row of stalls deep in the belly of the barn.

"Hello?" she called louder, the echo of her voice sending a chill down her back. Someone touched her side. She gave a start. Henry looked up at her. She expelled a breath.

From somewhere in the darkness a chain rattled, then something thumped against a wall. The faint sound of men's voices drifted out from the murky depths. Two figures emerged, walking side by side.

". . . take good care of that horse, heh? She is *caballo muy bueno*."

"I'll see to her doctoring right enough, Rodriguez. Next time, you just watch out where you ride her."

"Sí." He shook his head. "But the wire, she is not my fault. The wire, she was not there last year!"

Margaret saw them more clearly now—both tall men. One walked with a stoop, and as he passed by a lamp mounted to one of the timbers, the pale light reflected off his bald head. The other was heavier, wore a wide hat, and vaguely reminded her of the Mexican she'd met on the road to Baily.

"Hmmph. I got a feeling you're going to be seeing a lot more of that confounded stuff strung out across the range. Mark my word, Rodriguez, there'll be more torn fetlocks and crippled horses if men like you don't watch where they're riding."

"Hello."

The two men looked up.

"Ma'am?" the stableman said. "Didn't know no one was here." They came to the door, where the light was better.

The Mexican, though taller and not as heavy as the other man she'd met, had the same swarthy complexion. He wore his mustache neatly trimmed. A dark vest covered a red shirt, and a pair of overly long blue, pinstripe trousers bunched up at his black boots. His eyes were dark and mostly hidden in deep-set shadows, but his smile was friendly.

"I'd like to leave my animals for the night. They've had a long trip. Hopefully we'll be leaving tomorrow." How much was this going to cost her? She gritted her teeth, not wanting to speculate. Whatever it came to, she'd pay it. Once back home, she'd find a way to earn back all that she'd spent.

"Sure. I'll see to 'em." The stableman scratched his scalp and looked the animals over with a quick but experienced eye. "They'll be wanting a pail of grain, and some good grass hay. Got a long ride ahead of you, do you?"

"Yes. Carson. New Mexico Territory," she added in answer to his blank look.

"Oh, yeah, heard of it. That's a long ride." He scratched under his arm. "You didn't do it all in one day?"

"No. Two days." She smiled. "But I'm anxious

to get back. I hope to be able to leave in the morning, right after I speak with Sheriff Hawthorn."

He nodded and didn't question her business with the sheriff, though his widening eyes at the mention of Hawthorn's name was an open invitation to more news, if she'd be willing to give it. She wasn't. He turned to the Mexican. "Reckon I better run over to the pharmacy before Saunders closes up shop. I'll get that mare of yours back on her feet in no time."

"*Gracias, Señor* Farley." The Mexican doffed his hat to Margaret, revealing a thick black mop that should have made the stableman green with envy. "*Señora*. Have a *buen viage* back to Carson."

"Thank you, sir."

He grinned, tugged the hat back onto his head, and strutted out across the street.

The stableman turned back to her. "I need to run an errand over to the pharmacy, ma'am. Got an animal back there with a festering wound. That da—err, dadgum bobwire, you know!" His mouth screwed into a knot of disdain. "Soon as I get back with the salve, I'll see to your team. If you want, just pull your rig inside and leave 'em hitched."

"Thank you."

The stableman started off more or less in the same direction the Mexican had gone. She got back into the wagon and clucked the horses slowly into the dark belly of the barn, while Henry stood off to the side. She pulled the wagon far enough into the building to clear the sliding door, and set the brake. The faint light from outside barely reached past the wagon box, but there was enough of it that when the shadow flickered behind her, it caught her eye.

"Henry?" She peered over her shoulder. He was no longer standing in the doorway; and he wasn't in the shadows off to the side, either. She climbed down from the wagon seat. "Henry?" She scowled, and probed the deep shadows inside the barn, then cast toward the gloom gathering outside, but didn't see him anywhere. The day was still warm and the air inside the building held the sharp, pungent heat, but all at once she shivered. "Henry?"

Perhaps he'd wandered back to Francis's boardinghouse? She frowned. That seemed unlikely. The cold finger screwed itself into her spine again. She remembered Corely's shotgun under the seat and turned to retrieve it.

"I told you she couldn't stay away from me."

She gasped and spun around.

"Carson?" Johnson studied him with doubt in his deep-set eyes.

Now that Ketcham had given it a moment of thought, he knew it wouldn't play out. He shook his head, said, "It doesn't work," and looked down the road to Bailey, then back at the preacher. "Your wife said Ed MacRae saw Margaret turn east. Carson is west."

"You're second-guessing yourself, Ketcham. He that wavers is like a wave of the sea driven with the wind and tossed." Johnson dismounted and walked a few paces down the Bailey cutoff, his concentration once again on the road. "Go with your instincts. I think they're sharper than you're giving them credit."

Ketcham frowned. "What are you looking for?"

"This, I think." He hunkered down, picking at something in the road.

Ketcham swung to the ground stooped beside the big man.

"I've been shoeing the Mattlins' horses for nearly two years now. One of them has a narrow hoof. He got it caught in the cleft of a rock when he was but a colt. The deformity doesn't bother the horse, but it makes for a challenge fitting a shoe. A ways back I spied a track made by a horse not many hours ahead of us." His thick finger traced the outline in the dirt. "I can't be certain, Ketcham. Never claimed to be much of a tracker. But if I was a betting man . . ." He let his unfinished thought hang there for Ketcham to complete.

"It's more than we've had to go on so far, Preacher." He stepped back up into his saddle.

"And the boy?" Johnson gathered up his reins, swinging atop the tall horse.

Ketcham frowned. "There is only one way to know the answer to that. And we'll find it in Bailey." He put spurs to his horse and moved ahead.

He and Johnson rode into Bailey as dusk was settling over the town. Up and down the narrow street, lamps were being lit in saloons to show the way for the thirsty patrons drifting in off the cattle ranges.

"Where do you want to start looking?" Johnson said.

Ketcham eyed the open door of the Cattle King Saloon as they passed by. Piano music and the clicking of a roulette wheel drifted into the street. He licked his lips. There'd be a cold beer and a friendly game of cards in there. It was tempting, but more urgent matters weighed on him. He searched the faces of the men passing by. "We can start by asking around."

"In there?" Johnson was studying him curiously.

He hesitated. "No. Margaret wouldn't have any doings with a saloon."

Johnson said, "Someone in there might know Gellerman's whereabouts."

He frowned. "Let's hope she hasn't found Gellerman yet."

Johnson mirrored his concern. "How about in there?" He inclined his head toward a nearby building.

"A restaurant? It's a likely enough place to

start looking." They urged their horses toward the building wedged between a closed meat market and a darkened dry goods store.

He didn't hold out much hope of finding Margaret tonight. Being the sensible woman she was, she'd have found a room to spend the night by this time. The tinny music of the saloon called to him, but he resisted. First they'd ask questions in the restaurant. If that failed to lead them to Margaret, then maybe he'd wander into the Cattle King and ask some questions. And maybe have a beer.

The restaurant was busy. A woman using a cane came over to seat them.

"Just the two of you?"

"We're not staying," Johnson said. "We were just wondering if a woman and a little boy came in here earlier."

She eyed them suspiciously. "I don't recall."

"It's important," Ketcham said. "She may be in some danger."

"From the likes of you two, no doubt."

"So she was here," Johnson said.

The woman didn't answer. He and Johnson may have looked road-weary and disreputable, but he didn't have time for her evasiveness.

"How long ago did she leave?"

Her mouth tightened. "Just who are you?"

"Friends," Johnson said. "We're here to help Margaret . . . to bring her home."

Maybe she heard something in Johnson's voice

that convinced her. Her face softened slightly. "She was here. She left about an hour ago. Left in a big hurry. Left their food too, and it isn't that bad, mister."

"Where did she go?" Ketcham asked.

"Don't know. She'd asked about someplace to stay. I told her about Francis Kettering."

Johnson said, "Where would that be?"

"Far end of A Street."

Ketcham knew the place. They left and swung back onto their horses, starting for the corner.

"*Señor* Ketcham! You have come back!"

He reined to a stop and spied the Mexican standing on the sidewalk. "Rodriguez!" He turned his horse into the hitching rail and stuck out a hand. They shook. "How goes it, my *amigo*?"

Rodriguez fluttered a hand in the air. "Same thing every day. Work all the time. Come to town Saturday night and get drunk a leetle maybe. Then maybe dance with the *señoritas,* heh? And maybe other things too, if a man is lucky. Heh?" Rodriguez's face took on a more serious look. "But what are you doing back here? I thought I see the last of you, *mi amigo*."

"It's a long story. Me and my friend here, Reverend Johnson, we're looking for someone. A woman."

Rodriguez laughed. "*Sí,* aren't we all."

He didn't laugh. "It's not like that. This is a"—

he hesitated and glanced at Johnson, then back—
"a special woman."

"Oh." Rodriguez drew out the word, catching his meaning.

"Gellerman in town?"

"*Sí*, I see him earlier. Don't know where him is now. But Gellerman, him still *muy* angry at you, *mi amigo*. Stay clear of that one."

His gut tightened, not for his safety but for Margaret's. "I can't. He murdered the husband of the woman we've come to find. If she finds him first . . ." He shook his head, refusing to think of Margaret in Benny Gellerman's hands. His feelings for Maggie Mattlin had gone deeper than he suspected, and he was only now coming to realize how much she meant to him.

Rodriguez's dark eyes narrowed. "That sounds very bad. This woman, what does she look like?"

"Tall, young. Maybe twenty-five. Brown hair, blue eyes, a plain but honest face, and a pretty smile."

Rodriguez pulled at his chin. "Could be any woman, but I think maybe I see this woman. Not many new *señoras* in town. She travels with a leetle boy?"

Ketcham and Johnson exchanged looks. "Where?" Ketcham asked.

Margaret stared at the man who stood in the wide doorway, his face hidden in the shadows, but there was no mistaking Kit Wonderly or his leering voice.

A movement to Wonderly's left pulled her eye. Case McGruder stepped into view, his arm wrapped around Henry, a hand clasped over the squirming boy's mouth. "Appears you were right; it was her."

Kit Wonderly took a step. "Well, ain't you surprised to see me, Mrs. Mattlin? I can't tell you how pleased I am to see you." He started toward her.

Fear squeezed the breath from her throat. She took in a sharp gasp to clear it. "You stay away from me."

"Aww, you don't mean that. You might go and hurt my feelings. You and me together here in Bailey, it must be fate."

She glanced at the shotgun, an arm's reach away. "I'm warning you!"

"You're warning me?" He paused and laughed, but there was no humor in his voice when he went on. "I've been thinking about you a long time, Margaret. Ever since that social at the Grange Hall."

Her thoughts flew back to that night, the first time she'd seen Kit Wonderly. What foolish things had filled her mind, musings that had no place there. Not the way he had taken them. Not at all! But . . . she had wondered about a man so obviously reckless and dangerous.

"There was nothing in that? There never was."

"No?" He advanced another step. It seemed to her he was favoring his right arm, holding it stiffly. The faintly brighter light at his back still cast him in silhouette. "Maybe that's what you told yourself. Maybe it's what you told your man after you left. But I seen it in your eyes, the way you looked at me that night. You wanted me then, and I wanted you." Some of the shadows melted from his face in the flicker of a lantern.

No. She'd never wanted him. The very thought sickened her.

His pockmarked cheeks spread with a lusting smile. "Well, now's your chance."

Her chest felt bound by leather straps. Her view leaped between Kit Wonderly and Case McGruder. Mr. McGruder hadn't made a move, remaining in the doorway to bar her way if she somehow managed to dodge Kit Wonderly. Then there was Henry. She couldn't allow Mr. Mc-Gruder to harm the boy.

"Don't give me that frightened-doe look. You know you want it. How long has it been? Your husband's been dead for over a year. Or maybe you've been cozying up with Ketcham."

She gasped. Did those thoughts show too? Her curiosity, her penchant for dangerous men? But Chance wasn't dangerous, not like these men. Not evil. Oh, why had she left him and Corely? "I won't warn you again."

He threw back his head and laughed.

If she was ever going to do it, it had to be now,

while he didn't suspect. She grabbed for the shotgun and dragged it out from under the seat. Kit Wonderly stopped, staring at the twin barrels pointed his way.

"What do you intend to do with that, Margaret?"

"I'll use it if you make me." She glanced at Case McGruder. "Put Henry down."

He chuckled, a smug defiance in the tight twist of his lips.

"Tell him." She thumbed back one hammer and steadied the shotgun on Kit Wonderly.

Kit Wonderly was grinning. *Grinning!* His eyes, mostly hidden, shifted and focused past her left ear.

Someone grabbed her hand and yanked it away from the trigger. The shotgun was wrenched from her grasp, and she spun around. Benny Gellerman wasn't smiling, his face an expressionless rock.

Margaret seethed. "You!"

"Me."

His fist came up quick and hard, caught her in the stomach, and slammed her back against the wagon. She gasped for air, a wave of nausea washing over her, and tried to grasp for the wheel, but slid to the ground. Her brain reeled and her ears buzzed. Kit Wonderly's voice made its way past the bees.

"Easy or hard. It's up to you."

"There'll be a mite less fight in her now."

Benny Gellerman grabbed her by her shirtwaist and hauled her to her feet. Kit Wonderly covered her mouth with a sweaty grip.

Case McGruder tightened his hold on the squirming boy. "I don't know. I kinda like 'em with spunk in 'em."

She struggled for a breath.

"We'll each have our turn," Kit Wonderly said. "But she's mine first."

Her vision cleared. Three cold, calculating faces stared at her. The shotgun was still in Benny Gellerman's fist. He dropped the hammer and tossed it back into the wagon. "I know a place. The tack room in back."

She tried to bite the fist that covered her mouth, to break free of the arms that encircled her. But she was no match for Benny Gellerman and Kit Wonderly. A fist came from somewhere and clipped her chin, stunning her again. "Guess you want it hard," Kit Wonderly said. "Too bad, was hopin' we could *all* enjoy this."

"I'm going to enjoy what comes afterwards," Benny Gellerman said.

Kit Wonderly chuckled. "You bloodthirsty bastard."

They dragged her past the stalls. She couldn't scream, and she couldn't claw with her arms pinned, but she wasn't prepared to give up without a mighty fight. Struggling, she got a glimpse of Henry squirming in Case McGruder's grasp, he too being carried into the shadows. The boy was as helpless as she against these men. . . .

Case McGruder howled, and he fanned a hand. "The little bastard bit me!"

Or was he?

Henry stomped McGruder's instep. Case McGruder released his hold. Henry dropped to the floor, spun around, and threw a violent kick, planting the toe of his shoe in Case McGruder's groin. McGruder buckled, holding himself and groaning. Henry wheeled about and flew for the door.

Run, Henry!

Benny Gellerman lifted the rifle in his free hand.

Still gripping her mouth, Kit Wonderly barked, "Not here. Someone will hear."

Reluctantly, Benny Gellerman lowered the piece. He scowled at her. "You're not going to get away so easily."

Henry was away. They'd not hurt him.

Case McGruder sat upon the floor in the deep shadows, not moving, moaning softly. "He won't be interested in any of this in his condition." Benny Gellerman laughed, tightened his grip on her.

"Come on, let's get to it," Kit Wonderly said.

They dragged her deeper into the darkness.

Chapter Nineteen

"Her and her leetle boy, they were at the livery stable." Rodriguez pointed vaguely toward the edge of town. "But she will not be there still."

Ketcham knew the place. "Maybe not, but it's a start." He turned his horse away and headed for the corner.

"Ketcham!" Rodriguez called. "Wait for me." He caught up to them, walking a brisk pace to keep abreast of Ketcham's horse. "What is the hurry, heh? The lady, she is not going nowhere. Let me buy you and your friend a drink."

He had no thoughts of drink now. Find Margaret, give her a piece of his mind, then hug the breath from her. "Later."

The big building wasn't hard to find. He spied

it off to his left and another block down the side road.

Rodriguez, puffing, said, "Later? When have you ever said later to a beer, *mi amigo*?"

They were almost to the stable when a boy exploded from the big door, running wildly, shouting for help.

"There. That is the leetle boy I told you about."

Ketcham leaped from the horse and caught the child up in both fists. "What's happened?"

"They are hurting Mrs. Mattlin! In there! They are hurting her."

He thrust Henry into Rodriguez's arms. "Keep him here."

"Ketcham," Johnson's voice rumbled, "I think it's time for that rifle."

Ketcham yanked it from the scabbard and tossed it over his saddle to the big man, already in motion. Inside the dark barn, he stopped. A wagon was there—*her wagon*—the team still in harness. He'd found her! The sound of a struggle drifted faintly from someplace deeper inside. Fear mounted up within him a sudden dread that constricted the breath from his chest as he drew his revolver and turned the corner.

A row of dark stalls held half a dozen horses. They were skittish, as if something had recently spooked them.

"Margaret!"

Movement in the shadows to his right caught his eye. A man was sitting there, bent over with something in his hand. Ketcham threw himself to the ground as a gun boomed. In the orange flash that stabbed from the darkness, he recognized him.

McGruder? So where was Wonderly?

McGruder's gun roared again, and dirt stung Ketcham's cheek. The horses kicked at their stalls. He rolled into an empty one and fired at the place McGruder had been.

Johnson rounded the corner, hunched low, the rifle in his huge fists like he meant business. He pressed against the wall, his hulking form faintly outlined in the soft glow of a lantern.

McGruder scrambled behind a stall and snapped off another shot. The muzzle flash pegged his position. Ketcham and Johnson opened fire at the same time. When the thunder rumbled away, Ketcham leaped to his feet and dove across the narrow aisle. The echo of gunshots rang inside his head like a bell, and he strained against the sudden silence.

The struggling he'd heard earlier had ceased, and there seemed to be no sounds coming from McGruder's quarter either. He turned to listen to a scraping sound, like footsteps moving quickly. They stopped. The seconds ticked by.

"Ketcham." Johnson's deep whisper came from behind him. When he looked, Johnson jabbed the rifle barrel at the low ceiling over the stalls. The center portion of the barn soared to a high roof, its rafters hidden in the gloom up there, but directly over the stalls was the ceiling of the hayloft.

Ketcham nodded. He heard it too, the quiet footsteps creeping cautiously across the loft.

"McGruder. Throw out your gun." He waited. Behind him, Johnson dashed across the aisle, surprisingly nimble for a man his size, taking up a position in line with McGruder and the hayloft overhead.

Ketcham eased out of cover and slipped into the next stall up. A nervous horse sidestepped away from him. He put a gentling hand upon the animal's flanks. McGruder still hadn't made a sound. He crouched into the aisle and crept forward. Something caught his eye, and it took him a moment to draw it from the shadows into view. It was a boot heel, protruding slightly from a stall a dozen feet ahead.

It didn't move. When a few seconds had passed, he crept ahead again.

McGruder was sitting against a bullet-splintered wall, his gun still in his fist, his eyes wide and unblinking, staring at nothing. Ketcham let go of a breath and nudged him with the toe of his boot. The man toppled.

A sound from behind him spun him around. What he saw froze his lungs as cold fear grabbed his heart. Margaret's right eye was almost swollen shut. Blood streaked her chin and splattered her dress. The bodice of her dress had been ripped aside, exposing her arm and shoulder.

256

When he saw her like this, his fear suddenly thawed before the raging fire that filled him.

"Drop that gun, Ketcham. Drop it or Mrs. Mattlin will end up like McGruder." Wonderly pushed Margaret ahead of him, emerging fully from the shadows into view. He had an arm tight about her waist, his six-shooter pressed beneath her right arm. He came a few steps closer and stopped. Margaret appeared dazed. She staggered just to keep his pace.

He lowered the hammer on his Colt, bent, and tossed it away from him. "Let her go."

Wonderly exhaled sharply and gave a short, nervous laugh. "Not likely." He glanced at McGruder. "Him. Always telling me what to do. Like I was some kid or something."

He eyed the revolver pressed against Margaret's side. Somehow he had to draw Wonderly's ire to himself and away from her. "You are a kid. Men don't beat up women." If Wonderly was going to fire, it *had* to be at him.

A board creaked overhead. Wonderly's eyes shifted briefly, then came back to Ketcham. "Get over there, where I can see you better." He inclined his head toward the open floor. His gun was still hard in her side, and she squirmed.

Ketcham tensed. Wonderly was moving him to a place where his partner would have a clear shot. It had to be Gellerman. Stepping to the middle of the floor, he was careful not to glance at the loft, careful not to give anything away. He wondered briefly why Wonderly had hesitated at all. Could it be he didn't have a killer's heart? Was his threat to Margaret an act? He couldn't take that chance. Wonderly had tried to kill him at the stampede. He'd been a willing hand in his beating behind Ned Wheely's barbershop. And Ketcham had to believe he was prepared to kill here too.

"Is this where you want me?"

Wonderly didn't answer. He seemed to be waiting.

"It's where *I* want you."

Ketcham raised his eyes to the loft. "Benny." He fixed a smile to his face. "Somehow it doesn't surprise me you're in cahoots with the likes of these two." He looked to Margaret. Her eyes were wide, and moving now. She was aware of everything, although she gave no appearance of it, calculating the odds just as he was. *She'd be a helluva poker player. Ah, Maggie, so many surprises.*

"You slipped me once, Ketcham. You won't this time."

"What? You're going to kill me for forty dollars, Benny? Or is it because I whipped you in front of your friends? That's it, isn't it? I whipped you once and now you're going to whip me." He cast a quick glance to his revolver lying on the floor, judging the distance to it and his chances of reaching it before Wonderly or Gellerman filled him full of holes—him and Margaret.

"Something like that."

There was the sound of a commotion down the dark hall between the stalls. All at once the boy burst around the corner. He hauled up in the middle of the floor and shouted, "You leave her alone, mister!" Grabbing a hay fork, he charged.

Wonderly swung his gun.

"Henry!" Margaret turned sharply in Wonderly's grasp and drove a fist into his arm.

Wonderly grabbed at his arm and groaned, and Ketcham threw himself into the boy as he ran past, sweeping him up in his arms and shoving him into a stall.

Gellerman's gun roared. Ketcham rolled and snatched up his revolver. Margaret had become a wild animal, clawing Wonderly's eyes. He shoved her away, covering his face with one hand.

Ketcham fired. Wonderly lurched backward. A second shot spun him into a stall post. He shuddered as Ketcham's third bullet slammed him to the ground.

He remembered Gellerman overhead and leaped aside. The roar of a rifle and the sharp crack of the revolver resounded as a single shot. Gellerman tottered, then pitched over the edge and landed at Ketcham's feet. Johnson stepped out into the open, levering a fresh shell into the chamber.

Ketcham rushed to Margaret, picking her gently off the ground. She was limp as a rag doll, and he held her tightly in his arms. So he'd wait to give her a piece of his mind. Her arms encircled his neck, and she sobbed into his chest. He lifted her off the ground.

Johnson came over; his bulk a great shadow rimmed in light from the lamp behind him. "Is she all right?"

He felt her nod against his chest. "Yes . . . I think so."

Standing there a moment not moving, Johnson stared at Gellerman's body. Ketcham saw the frown and the way he looked at the rifle in his fist. Then the big man gave a small shudder and turned away, his shoulders slumped, his head bent.

Men began to pour into the barn. Rodriguez stood among them, looking embarrassed.

"I told you to keep the boy with you." The boy was looking worried, reaching to touch Margaret's arm.

Rodriguez shrugged. "The leetle brat, he kicked me." He rubbed his shin. "I ought to wring his scrawny neck."

"No one is going to wring anybody's neck." Ketcham carried her out of there. In the last of the daylight he saw the mess Wonderly had made of her face. "Dammit, Margaret!"

"I can't be that much worse than yours the last time." The spunk in her voice surprised him.

"But you're a woman."

"A woman alone."

"If you had told me, I'd have handled it." His grip about her tightened.

"I did tell you."

It was true. She'd asked for help and he'd told her he was moving on. He slumped. "Well, I'm a thickheaded fool. Next time, spell it out for me."

Her bruised lips tried to smile. "Will there be a next time, Chance?"

His gut cinched up like a trick saddle. "You need to be seen by a doctor." He glanced at the preacher. "Let's go, Johnson. Bring the kid."

Chapter Twenty

Ketcham crossed the parlor in three impatient strides, turned, and thumped his way back across the room.

"You're going to wear a path in Mrs. Kettering's carpet." Sitting in Frances Kettering's settee, Johnson looked like a giant in a roomful of furniture built for children. Although he hadn't stirred from the tight chair, his fingers had drummed a monotonous march upon the end table at his elbow.

Henry, hatless and brooding, fidgeted at the head of the hallway, staring down it at the door that remained closed.

A knock at the front door brought Mrs. Kettering across the parlor, eyeing them with a scowl as she opened the door. "Sheriff Hawthorn."

"Frances."

She stepped aside to let two men enter. Hawthorn was a tall man with fair skin, a full red mustache, and blue eyes. Ketcham guessed him to be about forty. He looked weary and in need of a shave as he removed his hat and glanced around the room, the soft flickering light from the colored glass lilies catching the nickel badge pinned to his gray vest. He wore a six-shooter and carried a leather packet under his left arm. He paused just inside the door, looked at her polished floor, and removed his spurs, setting them on the porch outside the door.

The other man was Jorge Rodriguez.

"Just get into town and Jorge here is waiting at my house to tell me there're three men down at Pemberly's parlor being fitted out for pine boxes. You the two responsible for Pemberly making his bills this month?"

From the sound of it, Hawthorn knew Gellerman well enough to waste little sympathy on the man. And if he didn't know McGruder and Wonderly, he at least had assumed that kindred dogs run in the same pack.

Hawthorn looked at Ketcham, then Johnson, then back, his eyes narrowing. "Do I know you?"

Rodriguez stepped past him. "*Sí*. This is *mi amigo*, Chance Ketcham. Ketcham him used to work for the Muleshoe outfit. And this is his friend, Father Johnson."

"Reverend Johnson," the big man corrected gently, remaining seated.

Hawthorn frowned, his view lingering momentarily upon the big man in the settee before shifting to Ketcham. "I got the story from three men so far—Johnny-come-latelies on the scene. Now I'd like to hear it from you two. I understand there was a lady involved. She suffered some injuries?"

"The doctor is in with her now." He inclined his head toward the hallway.

"Serious?"

"The doc hasn't been out." Margaret had said nothing when he carried her here to her rented room. She'd withdrawn. Maybe it was just the pain making talking difficult. Her eye had swollen shut and the bruises had begun to glow angrily by the time he'd placed her on the bed. Maybe it had nothing to do with her unanswered question, nothing to do with him. She had to be shocked and wounded by Wonderly's intentions. He would not consider past the man's intentions. He had to believe they'd gotten there in time.

The doctor had shown up soon afterward and shooed all but Francis from the room. Francis had reappeared a few minutes later to fetch hot water, saying only that the doctor was examining her.

As briefly as he could, Johnson told the whole

story, beginning with Hank Mattlin's murder. Henry added his part. Ketcham was grateful for their being there to fill in the details. His concentration was off, distracted by the closed door down the hall. Hawthorn took it all down on a tablet of paper he'd retrieved from his packet.

"Well, it don't surprise me Benny would get himself mixed up with this sort of thing." Hawthorn folded his tablet and tucked it back inside the portfolio. "From what I heard, and what you tell me, they got what they deserved. I'll talk to Doc Allen later about the lady's injuries. How long you two planning to stay in town?"

"It depends on what the doc says," Ketcham said.

Hawthorn pursed his lips and nodded, anchoring the portfolio back under his left arm. "I'll want to see you both in my office tomorrow." He shook his head. "This is gonna keep me in paperwork."

"We'll stay as long as you need us, Sheriff," Johnson said.

He nodded and turned to leave. Levering his hat back upon his head, he reached for the door, but looked back before opening it. "Hope the lady fares well."

"Thank you, Sheriff." Ketcham hoped the same. More than hoped—he'd even begun to pray about it, something he hadn't done in earnest since he was a boy. The sheriff left, and Ketcham resumed wearing out the carpet between the settee and the fireplace.

Of course she'd be all right. Banged up some, scared enough to never try it again . . . He paused his thoughts. No guarantee there. Margaret was a woman to follow her convictions wherever they took her. She needed a strong hand to keep her in line. Not Corely's, surely. He frowned.

When the door to Margaret's room opened, Johnson sprang from the settee, walking right behind Ketcham and Henry down the hallway. Dr. Allen shut the door behind him.

"How is she?" Ketcham asked.

"Resting." He motioned them back into the parlor. "Mrs. Mattlin will be fine. Which one of you two is her husband."

"She's a widow," Johnson said.

"Oh, I see."

"We're . . . friends." The word rolled stupidly off his tongue. It was not friendship he felt for Maggie Mattlin. *Wake up, Chance, your heart's jumped ahead of your brain.*

"Other than the obvious bruises and cuts, she has a fractured cheekbone. It should heal with no further treatment. She also has a couple broken ribs. I've bound them. Bed rest and taking it easy will heal those. She is in considerable pain, but she's young and strong."

Too strong for her own good. He clenched his hands. "Can I see her?" Maybe she'd tell him to

266

cut loose and ride out. If so, she'd have a fight on her hands.

"I've given her laudanum."

"Doc." He hesitated, uncertain how to ask the question. "Did they—"

"Violate her?" Allan finished, sensing his discomfort. "No, Mr. Ketcham. Thank God, no. You and Reverend Johnson arrived in time to prevent that maliciousness." Allen shook his head. "Animals. Some men are animals, Mr. Ketcham. Who's to explain it?"

Johnson folded his arms in front of him and scowled. "The explanation is easy, Doc. Tell a man he's descended from animals and that's how he'll act."

Doc Allen made a face like he'd bitten into a lemon. He thought it over and nodded. "You may be right, Reverend." He drew in a sudden breath and snatched his hat off the coatrack. "I will be by in the morning to check in on Mrs. Mattlin. In the meantime, try to see she isn't disturbed."

"Can I just look in on her?" Ketcham asked.

The doctor nodded. "Keep it brief."

He slipped quietly into the room and closed the door behind them. The air was warm, and heavy with the smell of antiseptic ointment. Margaret lay upon the bed, the left side of her face purple and puffed up, her left eye swollen shut, her skin glistening in the lamplight from the salve Dr. Allen had applied. In spite of her condition, she managed a fragile smile.

"Margaret." He stood there unsure of what he should say next. "The doctor says you'll be fine." He came around and stood beside the bed. Her one good eye followed him. "A few more days here and we can take you home."

"Corely will be madder than a wet cat." Her words were muffled behind thickened lips.

"No he won't. He'll be grateful just to know you're all right."

She touched her face. "I must look horrible."

"You look fine, Maggie." Seeing the bruises made him want to kill Wonderly all over again. It was wrong, but the feeling persisted. Then he realized the anger was toward himself. If he'd listened to her the first time, really heard her, he could have spared her this pain. He'd done the best he could confronting Ollfinger, focusing on the land, the chores, anything but Margaret and her heart's need. She'd wanted justice for her husband, probably loved him still. What was he doing going weak-kneed over the woman?

"You're going to need a lot of bed rest. I'll stay on and help Corely."

"You?" Her tone had an edge to it. "What about those greener pastures?"

He grimaced. "Thought I'd try lighting someplace for a change. See what it feels like to put down roots."

"Someplace?"

"Carson comes to mind."

"Why?" The edge sharpened. Even in her condition, she prodded him.

He wasn't going to make a fool of himself, admit to feelings she might not share. "I'd like to stay close to you and Corely."

A frown brought a wince of pain to her face. "The wanderlust would take hold of you again."

"Maybe. But I'd give settling down a real hard try . . . if I had a reason to."

She stared at him, her expression unreadable. Had he assumed too much, read more into her words than was really there?

"Roots put down are hard to pull up, Chance."

"Deep roots give oak trees their endurance."

Margaret watched him a moment. "Hank. He's been avenged. Justice has been served . . . hasn't it?"

He nodded. "Justice has been served."

"I . . . I need to put that behind me."

"If you can."

Her hand moved toward him, the smallest of gestures. He took it into his, feeling strength in that grip. Margaret was no halfhearted woman. But he was equal to it.

Ketcham fidgeted in the pew. It had been years since he'd been to a Sunday service and he still wasn't certain he liked the idea, but Johnson had been unrelenting, and it was the first Sunday Margaret was able to attend. Her face still showed the bruises deep beneath the skin, but they were disappearing.

She'd asked him to come. What could he say? Maggie was a hard woman to deny. These days he only wanted to make her happy, surprise that smile to her face.

From the pulpit, Johnson made a big thing of her recovery, eyeing both sides of the church as he spoke about the body's need for healing. The split across the aisle was dramatic, even to Ketcham, unused to such things. He, of course, sat with Margaret, Corely, and Henry on the farmer's side. The cowmen had all piled into the pews on their side. Both sides squirmed as Liam Johnson preached peace and reconciliation between God's people.

Collars became particularly tight, but Johnson didn't pull his punches. One part of the body could not war against another without weakening it all. It was the kind of sermon Ketcham could appreciate—sincere and honest.

Afterward, with folks filing out of church, Susan Johnson stopped Margaret and asked how she was feeling.

"I'm back to my work, and there is a lot of it to do. We've got that old barn torn down, and Chance and Corely are putting up a new one. And Henry's a big help too."

"Need an extra shoulder to haul timber?" a barrel-bottom voice asked. Johnson shook

Corely's hand, then took Ketcham's in his vise-like grip.

"Can always use a helping hand," Corely said.

"Especially one as strong as yours," Ketcham added.

"The first chance I get away from my forge, I'll be by." He looked down at Henry. "Any word from your pa, son?"

Henry shook his head.

Margaret placed a hand on his shoulder. "We'll keep sending wires and writing letters until we find him. Until then, Henry has a home with Corely and me as long as he wants it."

"Mattlin."

Corely looked over. Jeb Ollfinger came down the church steps, carrying his hat in his hand as he angled toward them. The cowman sucked in his paunch when he got near. He stopped, standing straight as a telegraph pole with his deep-set eyes bent down at Corely. His face might have been carved from a dried-up beam for all the expression it gave. He didn't smile, didn't speak for a moment. His gray hair shone in the late-morning sunlight like snow atop a craggy peak. His view glanced briefly off of Ketcham, then back to Corely. "Looks like you've taken on a hand after all."

"Nope. Ketcham's staying of his own free will."

"Own free will?" There was skepticism in his voice, and he looked at Margaret. "Ma'am, I'm pleased to see you're recovered." A grimace split the wooden face. "I'm only sorry it was men I hired who—who caused you such pain." Ollfinger cleared his throat, and Ketcham figured it the best apology they'd get from the proud man.

"I understand you have some of my cattle on your land."

Corely swallowed hard. "I do. Chance has been seeing to them."

Ollfinger considered Ketcham a moment. "You pointed out how I might be responsible for my men's . . ." He seemed to search for the right words. ". . . unnecessary zeal. Well, maybe there's some truth in that." He reached inside his suit jacket and withdrew a slip of paper, putting it into Corely's hand.

"What's this?"

"A bill of sale for those twenty-two head of cattle. It don't make up for everything you've lost, but the sale of those cows will get you through the winter."

Corely's mouth fell open.

"Thank you, Mr. Ollfinger," Margaret said.

"Ma'am." Ollfinger nodded, and without another word he returned to his wife's side, tugged his hat upon his snowy head, and helped Mrs. Ollfinger into their carriage.

"If that don't beat the shuck off July corn." Corely stared at the paper as the Ollfingers drove away.

Johnson chuckled. "Looks like you're a cowman, Corely."

Ketcham grinned. "Now, isn't that a pickle barrel? Next week you'll be having to choose which side of the church to sit on."

Johnson scowled. "Next week there won't be sides. If folks don't do it on their own, I'll assign seats like an old schoolmarm."

Ketcham laughed. He believed Johnson just would.

Corely gave an uncertain grin. "Corely's cows. How do you like the sound of that?"

Margaret took Ketcham's arm, her eyes bright and hopeful. "Not nearly as much as I like the sound of Ketcham's Land."

He liked the sound of that too. He had a fleeting glimpse of his own mother and father, working side by side on the land. It didn't look so bad after all, he decided as they walked to the wagon and drove back to the farm.

BRANDISH

DOUGLAS HIRT

FIRST TIME IN PAPERBACK!

Captain Ethan Brandish has finally given up his command of Fort Lowell, deep in Apache territory. But the vicious Apache leader, Yellow Shirt, has another fate in store for him. He and a group of renegade warriors attack a stage station and ride off just before Brandish arrives. But the Apaches are still out there—watching and waiting—and Brandish must risk his own life to save the few wounded survivors.

___4323-8 $4.50 US/$5.50 CAN

Dorchester Publishing Co., Inc.
P.O. Box 6640
Wayne, PA 19087-8640

Please add $1.75 for shipping and handling for the first book and $.50 for each book thereafter. NY, NYC, and PA residents, please add appropriate sales tax. No cash, stamps, or C.O.D.s. All orders shipped within 6 weeks via postal service book rate. Canadian orders require $2.00 extra postage and must be paid in U.S. dollars through a U.S. banking facility.

Name_____
Address_____
City_____State_____Zip_____
I have enclosed $_____ in payment for the checked book(s).
Payment <u>must</u> accompany all orders. ❑ Please send a free catalog.

Coyote Trail

John D. Nesbitt

Travis Quinn doesn't have much luck picking his friends. He is fired from the last ranch he works on when a friend of his gets blacklisted for going behind the owner's back. Guilt by association sends Quinn looking for another job, too. He makes his way down the Powder River country until he runs into Miles Newman, who puts in a good word for him and gets him a job at the Lockhart Ranch. But Quinn doesn't know too much about Newman, and the more he learns, the less he likes. Pretty soon it starts to look like Quinn has picked the wrong friend again. And if the rumors about Newman are true, this friend might just get him killed.

___4671-7 $4.50 US/$5.50 CAN

Dorchester Publishing Co., Inc.
P.O. Box 6640
Wayne, PA 19087-8640

Please add $1.75 for shipping and handling for the first book and $.50 for each book thereafter. NY, NYC, and PA residents, please add appropriate sales tax. No cash, stamps, or C.O.D.s. All orders shipped within 6 weeks via postal service book rate. Canadian orders require $2.00 extra postage and must be paid in U.S. dollars through a U.S. banking facility.

Name_____
Address_____
City_____State_____Zip_____
I have enclosed $_____ in payment for the checked book(s).
Payment <u>must</u> accompany all orders. ❑ Please send a free catalog.
      CHECK OUT OUR WEBSITE! www.dorchesterpub.com

Man From Wolf River

John D. Nesbitt

Owen Felver is just passing through. He is on his way from the Wolf River down to the Laramie Mountains for some summer wages. He makes his camp outside of Cameron, Wyoming, and rides in for a quick beer. But it isn't quick enough. While he is there he sees pretty, young Jenny—and the puffed-up gent trying to get rude with her. What else can he do but step in and defend her? Right after that some pretty tough thugs start to make it clear Felver isn't all too welcome around town. Trouble is, the more they tell him to move on—and the more he sees of Jenny—the more he wants to stay. He knows they have something to hide, but he has no idea just how awful it is—or how far they will go to keep it hidden.

___4871-X $4.50 US/$5.50 CAN

WILD ROSE *of* RUBY CANYON

JOHN D. NESBITT

At first homesteader Henry Sommers is pleased when his neighbor Van O'Leary starts dropping by. After all, friends come in handy out on the Wyoming plains. But it soon becomes clear that O'Leary has some sort of money-making scheme in the works and doesn't much care how the money is made. Henry wants no part of his neighbor's dirty business, but freeing himself of O'Leary is almost as difficult as climbing out of quicksand . . . and just as dangerous.

___4520-6 $3.99 US/$4.99 CAN

Dorchester Publishing Co., Inc.
P.O. Box 6640
Wayne, PA 19087-8640

Please add $1.75 for shipping and handling for the first book and $.50 for each book thereafter. NY, NYC, and PA residents, please add appropriate sales tax. No cash, stamps, or C.O.D.s. All orders shipped within 6 weeks via postal service book rate. Canadian orders require $2.00 extra postage and must be paid in U.S. dollars through a U.S. banking facility.

Name_____
Address_____
City_____ State_____ Zip_____
I have enclosed $_____ in payment for the checked book(s).
Payment <u>must</u> accompany all orders. ❏ Please send a free catalog.
       CHECK OUT OUR WEBSITE! www.dorchesterpub.com

WILL CADE

Larimont

John Kendall doesn't want to go back home to Larimont, Montana. He has to—to investigate the death of his father. At first everyone believed that Bill Kendall died in a tragic fire… until an autopsy reveals a bullet hole in Bill's head. But why is the local marshal keeping it a secret? John isn't quite sure, so he sets out to find the truth for himself. But the more he looks into his father's death, the more secrets he uncovers—and the more resistance he meets. It seems there are a whole lot of folks who don't want John nosing around, folks with a whole lot to lose if the truth comes out. But John won't stop until he digs up the last secret. Even if it is one better left buried.

___4618-0 $4.50 US/$5.50 CAN

THE GALLOWSMAN

WILL CADE

Ben Woolard is a man ready to start over. The life he's leaving behind is filled with ghosts and pain. He lost his wife and children, and his career as a Union spy during the war still doesn't sit quite right with him, even if the man sent to the gallows by his testimony was a murderer. But now Ben's finally sobered up, moved west to Colorado, and put the past behind him. But sometimes the past just won't stay buried. And, as Ben learns when folks start telling him that the man he saw hanged is alive and in town—sometimes those ghosts come back.

___4452-8 $4.50 US/$5.50 CAN

Dorchester Publishing Co., Inc.
P.O. Box 6640
Wayne, PA 19087-8640

Please add $1.75 for shipping and handling for the first book and $.50 for each book thereafter. NY, NYC, and PA residents, please add appropriate sales tax. No cash, stamps, or C.O.D.s. All orders shipped within 6 weeks via postal service book rate. Canadian orders require $2.00 extra postage and must be paid in U.S. dollars through a U.S. banking facility.

Name_____
Address_____
City_____ State_____ Zip_____
I have enclosed $_____ in payment for the checked book(s).
Payment <u>must</u> accompany all orders. ❏ Please send a free catalog.

Stalker's Creek
❧ WILL CADE ❧

Matthew Fadden's grandfather is the legendary Temple Fadden, a frontiersman nearly as famous as Davy Crockett and the subject of countless dime novels. But all Matthew inherited was a Henry rifle, with a stock custom carved by the old frontiersman himself. So when the rifle is stolen, Matthew isn't about to let anyone get away with it. He sets out to track down the thief, following a cold trail that leads him straight to the mining camp called Stalker's Creek, a place prone to trouble. Matthew certainly knows about trouble, but he's never seen anything like what's waiting for him in Stalker's Creek. But then Stalker's Creek has never seen anything like Matthew Fadden.

Dorchester Publishing Co., Inc.
P.O. Box 6640 ___5088-9
Wayne, PA 19087-8640 $4.99 US/$6.99 CAN

Please add $2.50 for shipping and handling for the first book and $.75 for each additional book. NY and PA residents, add appropriate sales tax. No cash, stamps, or CODs. Canadian orders require $5.00 for shipping and handling and must be paid in U.S. dollars. Prices and availability subject to change. **Payment must accompany all orders.**

Name: _____

Address:_____

City:_____ State: _____ Zip: _____

E-mail:_____

I have enclosed $_____ in payment for the checked book(s).

For more information on these books, check out our website at www.dorchesterpub.com.
_____ *Please send me a free catalog.*